George Cockings

War - an Heroic Poem

From the Taking of Minorca from the French to the Raising of the Siege of Quebec

by General Murray

George Cockings

War - an Heroic Poem
From the Taking of Minorca from the French to the Raising of the Siege of Quebec by General Murray

ISBN/EAN: 9783337213084

Printed in Europe, USA, Canada, Australia, Japan

Cover: Foto ©Andreas Hilbeck / pixelio.de

More available books at **www.hansebooks.com**

W A R :

A N

HEROIC POEM.

FROM THE

Taking of Minorca by the French,

TO THE

Raiſing of the Siege of Quebec, by General Murray.

By GEORGE COCKINGS.

L O N D O N :
rinted by C. SAY, in Newgate-ſtreet, for the AUTHOR;
1 Sold by J. COOK, behind the Chapter Houſe, St. Paul's
Church-yard. M.DCC.LX.

THE

PREFACE.

READERS, of whatever rank, or denomination, if ye fhou'd receive any pleafure from, and approve the following lines, as to their general defign, it is the fummit of my ambition. I am no writer by profeffion, but at my leifure hours, wrote the fiege of Louifbourg, in the winter of 1758: to amufe myfelf, and friends; and had no thoughts of printing it. But in the great and ever memorable year of fifty-nine, fo repeated, and rapid, were our conquefts, both by fea and land, in Europe, Africa, and America; fo often came news of our fucceffes from every part, (like gunpowder when

touch'd

touch'd by the match,) my fancy took fire! the rapt'rous joy grew too great to be contain'd within bounds! and I thought among the reſt, I wou'd add my ſhare of applauſe, and ſtrive to regiſter in the book of fame, the heroic actions perform'd by our troops and tars. I therefore aſſum'd my pen, and compleated the following poem : and being at length perſuaded by ſome gentlemen, (to whom I repeated it,) I have ventur'd it in the preſs, and ſubmit it to the public cenſure, from which there is no appeal ; and I hope they will look favourably on it, and not chill the ardour of my genius, by a ſevere criticiſm ; this being the firſt eſſay I ever dar'd offer to the public inſpection. Many faults, doubtleſs, may be found in the poem ; for I, perhaps, (like a tender mother, fond of her own offspring,) view it with partial prejudice ; and as ſhe can ſee fire, in a dull, languid eye, beauty, in a ruſtic freckled face, and ſymetry even in diſtorted limbs ; I fondly fancy a poetic fire glides thro' every part of it ; think

thoſe

thofe lines run fmooth, and fall with a proper cadence, which perhaps are rough and
diffonant; and tho' I fhould fancy a juft pro-
portion even in all its parts; where I think
it moft compleat, to others it may feem the
moft deficient. For the beft Gallic cooks, tho'
they are fo univerfally admir'd, cou'd never
yet, fend a difh to table, fo elegantly compos'd,
as to pleafe the palate of every feeder. How
then can I, unnotic'd and unknown, without
a patron, and unacquainted in this part of
England, and without the additional weight
of years on my fide: I fay, (all thefe circum-
ftances.confider'd,) how can I expect to give
a general fatisfaction, to the warriors, the wits,
the fcholars, and the men of fenfe; and to
every other clafs of readers, whofe fentiments,
doubtlefs, will not run concordant with my
own. But I have done all I can to give fatisfaction, and rouze a fpirit of emulation in
every reader. And if on the perufal, any
gentleman, that fhall find I have made any
material omiffions, will be fo good as to leave

a 4.   me

me a notice of it at Mr. John Cook's, book-
feller, behind the Chapter-Houfe, St. Paul's
Church-yard, and directed for me: if ever I
fhou'd be favour'd by the public approbation fo far, as to print a fecond impref-
fion, he may depend it fhall be inferted, fhou'd
the hint be fuitable to the defign of my poem.
But if it is a hint dictated by a party fpirit,
he may fave himfelf the trouble, and depend
it fhall never be inferted. For my intention
is not to calumniate any man, nor even to
write a true narration of what any particular
perfons may have done amifs, thro' cow-
ardice, inadvertency, inexperience, incautious
confidence in others promifes, pride, or the
like. Neither do I meddle with the intereft
of the two oppofing parties, in Great-Britain
and Ireland. But my fole defign is this;
(fir'd by a love of my country! and a generous efteem for all who have fought, bled, or
dy'd for my country's caufe!) to exert my
utmoft efforts, to inroll in the lift of fame
their names; to call them forth in the faireft
point of view; and drefs their amazing actions!

tions ! in all the elegance of harmonious numbers, and poetic truth ! to warm the heart of
him that fought and lives ! to give a juſt, de-
ſerv'd encomium, on the worthy warring
dead ! and inſpire with heroic ſentiments the
ſoul of every youth which reads, and hath not
yet been reaping the honourable harveſt of
martial glory !

He who governs his people with Regal
Lenity, and Paternal fondneſs : Thoſe who
hazard their Royal Perſons in battle for
their country's welfare : the Miniſters, and
Patriots, that nobly plan Her warlike ſchemes;
who firmly ſtem the tide of oppoſition, which
wou'd break down; and over-run the bounds
of her happy conſtitution; with all thoſe
who draw the ſword in Britannia's quarrel,
whether Engliſhmen, Caledonians, or Hibernians, and carry their patriot ſchemes,
dreadfully, into a waſting execution ! All ſuch
as theſe demand duty, allegiance, and a generous acknowledgment of every heart, ſen-
ſibly touch'd with a due ſenſe of their Kingly
care ! ſucceſsful plans ! and heroic perform-
ances !

ances! and such a King, such Princes, Patriots, and Ministers, has England got. And
such warriors we have, in the Royal Navy, and
Army of Great Britain, that common sense
and gratitude, bid us revere them ! and speak
of their great merits in the most exalted
strain ! and so long as I write, I shall always
bestow my encomiums on those, who plan
my country's good, preserve peace, and amity,
so much as possible in the land; fight her battles, and pour destruction on her inveterate
foes. These I say, shall employ my tongue,
to sing their fame, and give them due honours,
of what country or party soever : for he that
does the nation good, deserves a grateful acknowledgment of the same.

I have, as well as I can, thro' the whole
poem, preserv'd a continu'd narration of the
events, as they happen'd; yet I cou'd not avoid
interjecting some things, where they scarce
seem'd to claim a place: but as I thought they
scarce deserv'd discussion by themselves, I did
it to avoid a fruitless repetition of sieges, sur-
renders, attacks and skirmishes, and to keep
the

the poem from fwelling to too great a bulk. I mean thofe places in Africa, the Indies, &c. placing the time of their reduction, moftly at the time when the armaments failed from hence, deftin'd againft them; tho' in reality, they fell long after, beneath the heavy battle of thofe tars, and troops, which failed thither, arm'd with angry Britain's vengeance! For it was in lefs compafs than three years, the plans were form'd, and carried into execution, againft Louifbourg, the Continent, and Quebec: againft Maloes, Cherburg, and the Gallic fleets; and all the other expeditions againft our enemies in Africa, &c. So that I fcarce knew how to digeft the whole into a regular narration, and not vary in a point, as to the time of the events; and therefore I thought proper to throw in together the attacks and reductions of Guadaloup, Senegal, Granada, St. Martin's, Marigalante, Surat, Chandernagore, Calcutta, and the Nabob twice defeated; under the command of Watfon, Pocock, Moore, Clive, Draper, Marfh, Keppel, Mafon, Barrington, Sayer, &c. &c. &c. Thefe I therefore reckon'd up in the firft of the poem, when I mention'd

tion'd Great Britain rouſing to battle; Her armament for war, and pouring Her victorious
troops round about on every ſide; ſince it was
near about the ſame time they ſail'd from
England; and I hope as I have mention'd
ſuch events happen'd, and under ſuch Commanders, it will paſs without undergoing a
ſevere criticiſm. Whilſt General Wolfe, Admiral Saunders, &c. are beleaguering, and attacking Quebec; I have likewiſe mention'd
by way of epiſode, what General Amherſt,
General Johnſon, &c. &c. &c. atchiev'd on
the Continent; tho' perhaps, ſome of it was
done long before: but I ſcarce knew a place,
in which I cou'd inſert it more conveniently;
and I hope the learned Chronologer will let me
eſcape, without paſſing too harſh a cenſure on
that paſſage. And if I ſhou'd have tranſ-
greſs'd the rules of narration, in a ſeries of
ſuch great events, or deviated from the moſt
exact niceties, which ſome people may ima-
gine a work of this nature requires, I hope
the generality of my readers, of candour,
ſenſe, and learning, will put a favourable

con-

conftruction on it, and confider I am but
young, am no more than man; and therefore
very liable to great errors; and what a vaft
undertaking, for a youth's firft effay I have
now in hand.

I don't pretend to be a firft rate poet; perhaps may never deferve the title of a poet.
But I am confcious of my writing truth without flattery; unadorn'd with poetic fiction,
(which like a naufeous daubing on a beautiful
face, hides the fweet attractive fmiles, and
native fimplicity of the features:) and I
defign'd the poem for the honour of my
King and Country. And if my circum-
ftances wou'd have permitted that wafte of
time, and paying for paper, and the prefs,
without any thing for it, it wou'd have been
printed long fince; for I have delay'd it fome
time, on account of getting fubfcribers; and
have been favour'd with the approbation and
fubfcription of fome hundreds. I wifh I cou'd
keep pace in fmooth lines, and a nervous diction, with all the heroic actions perform'd
by

by the matchlefs warriors of the three nations;
whofe circumfpection in looking out for our
enemies, and conduct and undaunted bravery
in the day of battle, no pen can flatter. But
this is a thing only, to be wifh'd, and not to
be perform'd by the moft arduous application
of the great admirer of their deeds.

GEORGE COCKINGS.

THE

ARGUMENT.

WHILST others (in heroic, lofty verſe)
Great Fred'rick's name and Fred'rick's
praiſe rehearſe,
Mine be the taſk the Engliſh war to ſing,
Great Britain's heroes, and Great Britain's king.
By arms and battles gloriouſly inſpir'd,
(Replete with joy, with rapt'rous ardour fir'd)
I trace grim death, and our triumphant bands,
Thro' Indian, African, and Gallic lands ;
Where Engliſhmen, at martial glory's call,
Throng to the war, and ſcourge the plotting Gaul!
There Caledonians, (dreadful in their arms!)
Ruſh fearleſs on, 'midſt battle's loud alarms :
Thro' ranks of bay'nets, pikes, and hoſtile flame,
They hew the glorious path, to deathleſs fame!
Hibernians brave! with emulating glow!
Charge, pierce, repel, and chaſe the vanquiſh'd foe!

A 2   O'er

O'er ocean's fpace, my fancy wings its way;

Where GEORGE, the fecond, rules with fov'reign
     fway:

Thro' Neptune's realm, purfues our dauntlefs tars,

'Midft bluft'ring ftorms, and dreadful naval wars!

The genius of the nation, rous'd once more,

With vengeful thunder arm'd, they fhake the Gal-
     lic fhore!

GEORGE, WILLIAM, EDWARD, fwell the lofty ftrain;

GEORGE, who commands upon the azure main.

Like thefe, the lordly lions fpeed their way;

The fire firft roars, then fends his cubs to prey,

Next thefe ftands rank'd the fkillful Ligonier!

In battle brave! and to his fov'reign dear!

At Dettingen, (like Hector in the field,)

Hibernia's boaft; Britannia's faithful fhield!

Fierce in affault! (when young) matur'd w'th age,

A hoary hero! and a warlike fage!

Our patriots names, and merits, I proclaim,

To decorate the great heroic theme!

Who ftand unfhock'd, amidft the glorious caufe;

The Gallic dread! the props of Britifh laws.

Their

Their fouls, their fentiments, and their defires,

Incorporate, and mix like two bright flaming fires.

Bofcawen, Amherft, Hawke, (our Bulwark ftrong,)

Clive, Monckton, Saunders, grace the martial fong!

Brave Townfhend's . worth I fing: who fiercely
     fought!

And feiz'd the palm, a dying victor fought!

There Barrington, with Murray, brightly fhines!

Marfh, Mafon's, Sayer's names adorn the lines!

Holmes, Hardy, Watfon, Pocock, honour claim,

Who gain'd in diftant lands immortal fame!

Baird, Howe*, Speke, Lockhart, Keppel, are in-
     roll'd,

Rivals in fame, and naval warriors bold!

All who engag'd, where Hawke to conqueft flew,

Are regifter'd, with their encomiums due.

With thofe, whofe arms, the burnifh'd broad
     fwords weild;

Macpherfon, Frafer, Howe†, the terrors of the field!

Burton, whofe foul is full of active zeal!

---

  * Lord Howe, Capt. of his majefty's fhip Magnanime.
  † Col. Howe, who cleared the path, and diflodged the guards on the hill near Quebec; and when the two armies engaged covered the left flank and rear with his light infantry, from all attempts made by the French, Indians, and Canadians.

Dalling, and Ince, who fought for Britain's weal.

Each foldier fignaliz'd, each daring tar !

(The light'nings! and the thunderbolts of war!)

Thro' glory's paths, I ardently purfue!

But only write, what they alone can do.

Like radiant Sol, when at meridian height,

The heroes blaze with felf-refulgent light.

I fing how Wolfe, the faithlefs foe engag'd! ·

How, where he led, the battle fiercely rag'd!

The havoc of his war! the mould'ring walls!

Quebec's, Cape Breton's fate; the conquer'd
  Gauls !

His warlike deeds, no doubt, you'll all approve,

Whom vanquifh'd foes admire! and conq'ring
  Britons love !

By bloody toils, he earn'd, on hoftile ground,

That honour great; with which his mem'ry's
  crown'd !

In Britain's caufe, (amid the martial ftrife,)

He fought! he conquer'd! and refign'd his life!

So Sampfon flung proud Dagon's temple down!

Gain'd glorious death! and conqueft! and renown!

W A R:

W   A   R:

A N

H E R O I C   P O E M.

E patriots fage! who plann'd the
deep defigns
Of war: 'midft which Britannia
dreadful fhines!

(On whom fhe leans, with great exulting glow!

Where'er you point, fhe ftrikes the wafting blow!)

Ye mighty warriors! terrors of the world!

By whom, at land, and fea, our thunder's hurl'd!

To you this book is fent, with filial fear;

Craves foft'ring fmiles; and begs paternal care.

You, who like David's worthies, round the throne

Of mighty GEORGE, form a tremendous zone!

From

From you the tranfpórts flow ! 'tis you infpire!

As bluft'ring winds to flame blow latent fire !

From you I caught the great refiftlefs glow !

Whilft you dealt veng'ance on th' infulting foe !

Whilft you, on land, the pride of Gaul reftrain !

Or fweep victorious o'er the fwelling main !

My fancy burns ! tranfported with delight !

With ardour wing'd ! purfues you to the fight !

So few in years, my life, (without efteem ;)

I have no patron for the glorious theme !

Oh ! prop the caufe of honour ! fame ! and truth

Cherifh the fallies of unripen'd youth !

Since from your deeds, the growing theme muft rife

Accept the tribute due, and deign to patronize.

When I at firft poetic ardour knew,

And big with martial themes my bofom grew !

From pregnant fancy, (fir'd by warlike worth)

My rifing thoughts prepar'd to fally forth

In years a child, in litt'rature more young ;

With fecret tranfport on the theme I hung !

I heard much talk of Dettingen's fam'd fight,

Where Lewis bow'd beneath the lion's might.

Grown more mature, (a manly age attain'd)

The strong impreffions on my mind remain'd.

I wifh'd a day like that, to grace my pen,

When GEORGE the fecond fought at Dettingen ;

Whofe prefence banifh'd all defponding dread,

And thro' the ranks an emulation fpread :

Whilft brave Auguftus, from his royal Sire,

Caught the great flame, and burn'd with martial
      fire ;

Methought I trod the glorious fanguin'd way ;

When Cumberland pierc'd thro' the French array!

Sometimes I view'd intrepid Ligonier!

Plunging thro' deaths ! and void of grov'ling fear!

GEORGE ftood like Jove amid a thunder-ftorm;

Like bolts and light'nings thefe the Gallic ranks
      deform.

The triumphs and the terrors of the fight

Rofe to my view, and play'd acrofs my fight.

Quick thro' the chafe my flying fancy fped,

When gens d'armes, and main corps, in pannic
      fled.

Headlong

Headlong they drove! afraid to ftop for breath!

Rufh'd thro' the Rhine, and plung'd to watry
death!

Colours deferted, 'mongft the wounded lie;

And Gallic ftandards wear a purple dye :

Guns, pikes, fpontoons, in wild diforder fpread,

Promifcuous lie among the num'rous dead:

Drums, horfes, chiefs, riv'd helms, and fpouting
brains!

Breaftplates and loathfome carnage load the plains.

So the fam'd field of Dettingen appear'd,

With Gallic troops beftrew'd, with Gallic blood be-
fmear'd.

Juft as I reach'd the years to mark me man,

The prefent war to burn a-frefh began ;

Defign'd, no doubt, by ftrong refiftlefs fate,

To fling proud Gallia from her high eftate.

When Wolfe and Amherft, with Britannia's hoft,

Defcended on Cape Breton's hoftile coaft;

Now firft my heart conceiv'd the great defign,

Whilft thefe two heroes mightily combine

To

To fink or burn the fleet, and raze the walls,

Of Louifbourg,, with Britain's bombs and balls.

When Maloe's fleets, in Englifh flames expir'd;

The burning news my teeming fancy fir'd:

I trac'd prince EDWARD clofe to Cherburg's wall,

And faw the pride of France before him fall:

My raptur'd bofom, big with pleafure grew;

When Bofçawen oppos'd, and beat De Clue.

Who fhrank, o'erpow'r'd from his impetuous fire,

And left his Ocean * in the flames t'expire;

But oh! who can the wond'rous glow difclofe,

When Hawke (by tars efteemed) beat Britain's

    foes?

Whilft he with rapid flight to conqueft flew,

Conflans transfix'd, devoid of courage grew;

He led the van, the rear, and center run;

And England's fire devour'd the Royal Sun †!

As in his foul, who clafps the yielding fair,

The mighty tranfports roll beyond compare,

My joys rufh'd in like a tumultous flood;

The pond'rous pleafure trill'd along my blood:

  * Monf. De Clue commanded the fhip Ocean.
  † Le Soleil Royal. The fhip Monf. Conflans commanded.
In Englifh the Royal Sun.

When

When certain news arriv'd to glad our land,
(Which shall unparallel'd for ages stand)
Our troops had giv'n the num'rous Gauls a check,
And Townshend had possession of Quebec ;
Like rocks, amid the fight, our warriors stood ;
Death conquer'd Wolfe ! but Wolfe Quebec sub-
    du'd :
All these events, and more, my breast inspir'd ;
By warmth unknown before my soul was fir'd :
To sing th' exploits Britannia's sons have done,
What wonders they've perform'd, what mighty
    battles won :
Can I, whilst they victorious onward roll,
In nervous thund'ring diction trace the whole ?
Who can the wond'rous worthy task perform ?
Speak as they fight, or write as when they storm ?
The task, the toils of Hercules exceeds ;
Phæton as well might drive Apollo's steeds :
Now for old Homer's flight, and Homer's fire ;
Come Homer's soul, and all my soul inspire :
Thy strong conceptions with my fancy blend,
Like thine, the task is war! like thine the theme
    must end !   Oh!

Oh! might a portion now of Whitehead's fkill!
Or Mafon's fire, 'my glowing bofom fill:
Might Jóhnfon's genius in my foul prefide,
Direct, fuggeft, and my invention guide:
The flacken'd reins to fancy's flight I'd give,
And in immortal lines each hero's name fhould live!
But fate denies what reafon bids me afk;
Youth immatur'd, muft grapple with the tafk:
A pond'rous tafk, but 'tis a glorious aim;
My fancy's fir'd amid the warlike theme.
And as the clangor of the trumpet's found
Makes the fierce horfe with fury paw the ground;
A gen'rous ardour trills along his veins;
To glory's goal he fcours the fanguin'd plains:
So I, well pleas'd, fair honour's call obey,
Sing Britain's triumph, and the Gaul's difmay.
Of Providence and Britain's happy ftate,
By heav'n preferv'd from black impending fate;
This be my theme, this be my fweet employ;
To fing the ftrain with great enrapt'ring joy.
Clio! Urania! guide me thro' the whole;
And with cœleftial ardours fill my foul:

In

In nervous diction, teach my tongue to fing,

Great GEORGE, victorious, Britain's much lov'd King.

To tell how EDWARD, BRUNSWICK's grandfon,
    fought;

And Howe, and Marlb'rough, Britain's vengeance
    brought

Round Maloe's walls, mute guns, and troops in
    fright;

Whilft fleets afcend in air, 'midft blazing night!

Set Wolfe, Hawke, Amherft, Bofcawen, to view;

Speak all their worth, and give them honour due:

With Schomberg, Rogers, Johnfon, greatly fam'd,

Let Monckton, Townfhend, Keppel, Clive, be
    nam'd.

To Indian climes conduct my fancy far,

To trace the fons of Scotland through the war:

Difplay the prowefs of that martial race;

And in true light their matchlefs valour place.

Bring ev'ry Britifh hero on the ftage,

By patriot ardour fir'd, and manly rage,

Who dar'd in Britain's caufe againft the foe
    t'engage.

Rouze

Rouze me to trace 'em thro' each fierce alarm !

With martial fentiments, my bofom warm !

Teach me to fing, their dread voracious frowns,

In flaming death ! thro' Gallic troops, and towns !

Oh ! give me ardour ! fuch as well may fit

The fortitude, and eloquence of Pitt,

His name, a place, moft worthily may claim,

To aggrandize the pleafing warlike theme ;

That Pitt ! which Gallic lines cou'd never found !⎤

Greatly capacious ! wond'roufly profound !   ⎬

Where Lewis, and his politicks are drown'd ! ⎦

There all his treafures of the torrid Zone,   ⎤

With northern furs, forts, fettlements, are thrown ! ⎬

There funk Quebec, to grand deftruction down ! ⎦

A vaft exulting glow, my bofom warms !   ⎤

For heav'n, propitious, profpers Britain's arms ! ⎬

And mighty Fred'rick's name, the quadrate league ⎟

    alarms !   ⎦

GEORGE fills the throne, and governs well thefe⎤

    lands ;   ⎟

Next him, with manly foul, great Pitt commands ; ⎬

And on a Legge well fix'd, moft firmly ftands ! ⎦

So many, giant-like, of late have rofe,

And dealt with patriot zeal, 'gainft Gaul their blows!

Have acted like the hand of mighty fate,

To prop the throne, and fave the Britifh ftate !

As ftands the man, o'erwhelm'd with dazzling light,

The oculift hath juft reftor'd to fight :

Around he looks, abforp'd in dear amaze !

And new born blifs, midft bright Apollo's blaze !

With glorious tranfports ! wonders he furveys,

His Maker's Hand, Omnipotent, difplays!

So view I Royal GEORGE, with conqueft crown'd,

Whilft throngs of heroes brave ! his throne fur-
　　　round,

In pleafing joy ! and grand reflection drown'd !

Homer, his great Achilles much extoll'd,

And in the lift of fame, a few inroll'd ;

Exprefs'd a grand luxuriance of thought,

When he each hero into action brought ;

And with heroic fkill, the great narration wrought.

But had he liv'd in GEORGE the Second's days,

A deathlefs monument of fame to raife

For ev'ry hero we in Britain find,

The tafk would grow too great for Homer's mind.

All

All, cannot with diftinguifh'd merit fhine,

Cohorts muft throng, in one great pleafing line ;

And fleets, in compafs of a fingle page,

Attack, repel, and quell the hoftile rage.

WHEN

WHEN firſt th' unwelcome news to us was known,

The Gallic thunder fell on Portmahon;

As mourns the mother (fond,) her offspring's cries,
Who craves her aid, from threat'ning danger flies,
Maternal doubts, and ardent wiſhes riſe.

So mourn'd each Briton true, Minorca's fate,

Approaching near, and imminently great!

At length, the thund'ring news reach'd Britain's coaſt,

Our ſquadron fled, and Portmahon was loſt !

Reports came thick, the French prepar'd to land,

And ravage England, with a mighty hand;

Their threat'ning troops, to fancy ſtrong appear'd,

And ſighs, and pray'rs, and ſad portents were heard!

Gallia,

Gallia, with conqueſt fluſh'd! pronounc'd our doom,

And England ſeem'd involv'd in horrid gloom !

(As children with a bugbear tale are ſcar'd,

So we, of fleets, and troops, affrighted heard!)

E'en like the ſun, forth burſting from a cloud,

(With lightning ſtor'd, and ſtormy tempeſt loud;)

To glad the traveller in lonely ways,

And ſhed around, his ſweet all-cheering blaze,

Now Pitt aroſe, to glad our mournful iſle,

Diſpell'd the gloom, and made Britannia ſmile !

The ſcandal of the nation ſoon was raz'd,

Th' inſulting foe retir'd, transfix'd! amaz'd!

Before his eloquence, black perfidy was chas'd!

He plann'd the war! and practis'd martial ſchemes!

And waken'd Lewis from his conq'ring dreams !

Now like a lion rouſing from his den,

(To meet the dogs, and animating men;)

Who ſees his cub lie ſprawling on the ground,

Whom hungry dogs, moſt greedily ſurround:

B 3   He

He shakes his mane, and from his wrathful eyes,

Indignant fire, in dreadful glances flies !

Horrid he roars ! and swings his mighty tail,

For grand revenge, prepares both tooth and nail:

Foaming, he views the lacerated spoil ;

(Hunters, and dogs, and horses, back recoil !)

So England rous'd, on fell revenge inclin'd :

'Gainst Maloes, Cherburg, Louisbourg design'd ;

As if one soul did ev'ry Briton fire,

All rush to arms, and burn with wrathful ire !

Now o'er the main, our fleets assert our right,

Round Britain's standard, with a stern delight,

Troops throng on troops, and wish the rumour'd

     fight!

With free-born rage, all animated stand,

At danger spurn, and dare the foe to land:

Wives, children, laws, and liberty's sweet charms,

With threefold ardour ev'ry bosom warms !

Now Watson, Sayer, Barrington arose,

Roar'd in the storm ! and crush'd Britannia's foes !

                          Clive,

Clive, Marſh, and Maſon, Draper, Keppel, Moore,
To Africa, and India, veng'ance bore;
Theſe, with more brave commanders thither ſail'd,
With mighty hand, againſt our foes prevail'd.
Like hurricanes, and earthquakes, forc'd their way,
Made nations bend, and own great GEORGE's ſway!
Reliev'd Madraſs, repair'd its batter'd wall;
Triumphant ſeiz'd on ſwarthy Senegal!
Their cannon ſhook devoted hoſtile ground,
And ſcatter'd deaths,'mongſt faithleſs tribes around!
They ſtood transfix'd! their vital blood ran cold!
Whilſt England's ſtorms, o'er towns, and ramparts
    roll'd!
Houſes, and walls, from their foundations ſtray'd,
And pil'd in ſmoaking waſte, o'erwhhelm'd the
    blaſted dead!
Granada now, St. Martin's, Guadaloup,
Beneath Britannia's might, ſubmiſſive ſtoop!
Marigalante, Surat, Chandernagore,
Calcutta trembled, whilſt Clive's thunders roar!

*Clive! by whofe might, Chandernagore * was raz'd,

Before whom twice, the Nabob fled * amaz'd!

Clive! whofe impetuous war, bore down his foes!

Clive! who made Nabobs *! Nabobs * cou'd depofe!

This adds a luftre to great Brunfwick's throne,

His gen'ral † does, what conq'ring Rome has done.

Victorious oft! for battle greatly fam'd!

By Africans, The never * to be conquer'd nam'd!

(Tho' with more fhips, by thoufands better mann'd,

Enough to make pale fear itfelf to ftand;)

Thrice fled D'Ache, when dreaded Pocock came,

'Midft Englifh tars, and fheets of Britifh flame!

Now Englifh worthies, on the continent,

Made Indian-French, and favages repent

Their cruel, black, infernal, fcalping rage,

Not daring with our free-born troops t'engage;

***** Calcutta, and Chandernagore, were taken by Gen. Clive, the Nabob was twice defeated by him; and Jaffier Ali Cawn made Nabob. The people in that country, gave him a name, which in their language fignifies 'The never to be conquer'd.

† The Romans would often depofe one king, and raife ano·ther; General Clive depofed the Nabob, and raifed another to that dignity.

(They

They fought in fear, or fled in foul difgrace,
As tim'rous deers, when angry lions chafe.

Not fatiate fo, on ampler veng'ance bent,
Againft Cape Breton, England's fleet is fent.
Behold, they come! off Louifbourg appear;
Their coming ftrikes with an ámazing fear!
Pale tremor fills French forts, and troops, and
      towns,
And fcalping crews, for angry Britain frowns!
And like Briareus *, with an hundred hands,
She feiz'd on African, and Indian lands,
And pour'd around, her brave victorious bands!
Onward they roll'd, like an o'erwhelming flood!
And delug'd Gallic lands, in Gallic blood!

The French invafion now, is fear'd no more,
Our troops prepar'd to tread the Gallic fhore:
On ev'ry fide, their angry blows they dealt,
St. Maloes firft, their vengeful fury felt!

* A hundred handed giant, as the poets fay.

The

(The French flat bottom'd policy repaid,

Heav'n fent the Pruffian Hero to their aid.)

There, before Britain's troops, by Marlb'rough led,

On friendly ground, the tim'rous Frenchmen fled;

Whilft under covert of St. Maloe's wall,

Whole fleets of fhips, an eafy conqueft fall.

Six fcores their number, (needlefs are their names,)

A prey, to Britain's dread voracious flames!

As from on high, the tow'ring eagles ken

The ferpent's brood, before the female's den;

Downward they foufe, and feize the fcaly prey,

In griping talons, fafely born away.

(They mock the mother's hifs, with gen'rous fcorn,

Aloft in air, the venom'd brood is born;)

So Howe, and Marlb'rough, jointly fped their way,

And boldly feiz'd upon the Gallic prey!

Greatly refolv'd, the neighb'ring forts they dare,

Whilft hoftile wealth evaporates in air!

A3

A S daring Louifbourg, our navy lay,
Stretch'd off, and on, upon the fwelling fea;
It pleas'd the hand of heav'n to interpofe,
And fend on Britain's fleet its ftormy woes ;
'Caufe Louifbourg, as yet, not ripe for fate,
Muft be preferved to a longer date.
A heavy gale, at firft, the fleet divides,
The rolling waves, dafh'd hard againft their fides !
A tempeft next, with fury uncontroul'd,
High o'er their decks, the furging billows roll'd!
The foaming ocean madly round 'em rag'd !
A hurricane, the Britifh fleet engag'd !
Each fhip was now in danger to be loft,
The ftorm urg'd hard, upon the hoftile coaft ;
Still grew more ftrong, and louder than before,
And forc'd our fleet upon the Gallic fhore.
No longer now, they cou'd the fury brave
Of wind, and ev'ry pond'rous dafhing wave!
Towards the fhore, in grand confufion ride !
Born on the back of the tumultous tide.
As vapours vanifh in the fpacious air,
The angry winds, the fpreading canvas tear !

Halliards,

Halliards, and ſtays give way, like burning tow ! ⎫
Yards, topmaſts, blocks, a pond'rous burden grow ! ⎬
With craſhing noiſe, come tumbling down below ! ⎭

Wave, after wave, rolls over the quarter-deck,

Sweeps fore and aft, and threats each ſhip with wreck !

Amid the waves they plunge ! again they riſe

On watry hills, and ſeem to greet the ſkies !

High o'er the windward ſide, proud billows come,

To leeward roll, in froth, and briny foam !

Each tumbling ſhip, now ſallies as ſhe glides,

And in the ocean dips her lofty ſides !

Lan-yards, main-ſhrouds, and chain-plates go to ⎫
     wreck,   ⎬
The lower maſts, are ſhorten'd to the deck !   ⎪
And from their breechings, heavy cannons break ! ⎭

To ſtop the guns, hammocks are quickly flung,

And now, the heavy unſtay'd boltſprit's ſprung !

A damp, now chills the boldeſt ſeaman's, ſoul,

As they drive on, and in the tempeſt roll !

The danger now, ſeems greater than before,

For juſt a-lee, behold the Gallic ſhore !

Captains,

Captains, lieutenants, boatſwains, vainly rave, ⎫
In vain, the hardy tars, the tempeſt brave; ⎬ .
The ſhip's impell'd by each impetuous wave! ⎭

Amid the tempeſt, human ſpeech is drown'd,
From ſtem, to ſtern, nought but confuſion's found!
Whilſt ſome, (perhaps) are floating on the ſea,
Waſh'd from the decks, or blown with yards away.
Anchors, are now the only hope that's found,
Yet oft, they furrow up the faithleſs ground.
The Tilbury, no longer can ſuſtain
The rough aſſault of the tempeſtous main :
Her cables parts, whilſt angry tempeſts roar,
And like a horſe unbridled, leaps on ſhore !
There ſoon became, a diſmal ſhatter'd wreck,
The maſſy beams, and ſolid timbers break;
Bolts, trunnels, ſtaples, knees, and all give way,
The floating ruin ſpreads the ſurging ſea !
High o'er the ſhip, the foaming tempeſt laves !
And Britiſh ſeamen ſink in wat'ry graves !
Powder, deſign'd in thunder to diſplode,
Sinks down, oppreſs'd, with an aquatic load,

Is

Is now expended on the Gallic fhore,

In other noife, than when loud cannons roar.

Indulgent Heav'n at length, the ftorm appeas'd,

Of all their fears, the Englifh fquadron eas'd :

The foaming furges, wear a fmoother form,

God nodded peace! and filent grew the ftorm!

Half wreck'd! difmafted! in a difmal fort!

Our fleet foon anchor'd in a friendly port;

From whence to England, back again they plough,

And Britons mourn'd the ftormy overthrow.

STILL, like a loaded thunder-cloud, from far,
Great Britain growl'd revenge, and flaming war !

England, ftill ruminates, to Gallia's dread,

On veng'ance ftern, and ruin widely fpread !

Minorca's fall, for great reprifals cries;

She views Cape Breton with revengeful eyes !

So ftorm'd Achilles, his Patroclus loft,

And ey'd great Hector mid the Trojan hoft.

He grafp'd his fpear; he pois'd his pond'rous fhield;

Compleatly arm'd, again, he took the field!

His

His teeth he gnafh'd, and with a mortal frown,

Thin'd Trojan ranks, and mow'd their warriors
    down.

Beneath his blows, the tim'rous Dardans yield,

And godlike Hector, breathlefs loads the field!

At length, thewifh'd-for fpring, once more appear'd,

And Bofcawen, the Britifh banners rear'd :

The glad'ning news, with pleafure fill'd each mind,

Great George, a fecond northern war defign'd !

Englifh, Hibernians, Scotchmen, now are fhipt,

With all accoutrements for war equipt !

With brazen mortars, whence the bombs are flung,

And congregating fleets together throng :

The pond'rous batt'ring guns are put on board,

With barr'd, and round fhot, fhips are largely ftor'd !

With bombs, tents, horfes, (fit to draw the car,)

And all the apparatus of the war ;

With loads of footy grain, to fling the bombs from
    far !

Our fleets refitted, o'er the billows ride ;

(The dread of France! and Britain's naval pride!

Widely

Widely they fpread, upon the fwelling fea,

And thro' the weftern ocean fpeed their way ;

The dreadful pomp, of threatning war difplay !

Heav'n fmil'd th' affent, and back they ne'er return'd,

Till batter'd Louifbourg, in flaming ruin mourn'd!

Behold they come, with friendly fquadrons meet,

Retard, and intercept the Gallic fleet :

Widely they ftretch along the hoftile coaft,

Not long, e'er Lewis mourns this ifland loft.

A council's call'd, where meafures they propofe,

Where beft to land, where moft annoy the foes ;

Brave Bofcawen, (like Ithaca's* fage king,)

The hinge, on whom, the grand defign muft fwing,

Wifely forefaw, (and ponder'd in his mind,)

Unlefs our troops, unanimous combin'd,

The whole defign, might foon abortive prove,

As that, where Moab†, Seir†, and Ammon† ftrove.

* Ulyffes, king of Ithaca, was a Grecian king, and warrrior, at the fiege of Troy, and much renowned for his fagacity, and fkill in carrying on a warlike fcheme.

††† 'Tis faid in fcr pture, when the children of Moab, Am-
mon, and Mount Seir, came againft Ifrael, a diffention arofe
among the troops, they drew their fwords, attacked, and deftroyed one another; and by that means, defeated their own defigns againft the coafts of Ifrael.

First

Firſt diſcontent, next martial anger burn'd,

Each drew his ſword, againſt his ally turn'd;

England too oft, the like miſhap hath mourn'd!

But Boſcawen, of large and gen'rous ſoul!

So well projeȼted, and contriv'd the whole,

That Engliſh, Scotchmen, and Hibernians bear

Of fame, and danger both, an equal ſhare.

To his ſage conduȼt we may chiefly owe,

The French repuls'd, with rapid overthrow!

Now all prepar'd, (the landing place in view,)

For ſev'ral days a bluſt'ring tempeſt blew:

Which for that ſpace, the bold attempt retards;

But Providence, the Britiſh frigates guards;

For tho' they rode full near the hoſtile ſhore,

And Gallic cannon, with inceſſant roar,

And tho' briſk fire from mortars was maintain'd,

Small was the loſs, or damage they ſuſtain'd!

Again, the wind, and waters, ceas'd to rage,

And now, the fleet, and troops, prepare t'engage;

Now line of battle ſhips approach the ſhore,

And nearer ſtill, the leſſer frigates roar!

C   Againſt

Againſt th' oppoſing foes, a dreadful bar!

Whilſt tranſports quick refund the living war!

Tumult! and noiſe! and ſlaughter! quick enſu'd,

And men, and boats, are daſh'd upon the flood!

Cannons inceſſant roar, and bullets rend,

Down thro' the air, the countleſs bombs deſcend!

And ſulph'rous flames, and clouds of ſmoke ariſe,

Whilſt from French infantry, the leaden bullet flies.

Mean while, our frigates, cannons, mortars ply;

And bombs, and balls, in deadly volleys fly.

Amherſt, and Wolfe, proceed, ſerene, ſedate,

As if themſelves had turn'd the hinge of fate:

By them inſpir'd, our infantry ſoon grew

With ardour warm, and to the battle flew!

Bore all before 'em, like the ſwelling main,

The French could not their mighty charge ſuſtain!

Expanding ſheets of vapours cloud the day,

Whilſt boats to land (with ſpeed,) purſue their way.

See! ſee! the crimſon blood, brave Bailly ſtains;

The (glancing) leaden death, hath pierc'd his brains!

The manly Cuthbert's merit well is known,

Who fondly cry'd, my Bailly! dear! you're gone!

Oh!

Oh ! fad ! there ftopp'd the amicable breath !

Brave Cuthbert felt the dafhing iron death !

The fatal bullet, through his body came ;

And drown'd in blood, the glowing friendly flame.

From Scottifh warriors, tears of anger flow !

Their bofoms glow'd with pond'rous martial woe;

For Cuthbert oft, and Bailly, brav'd the foe.

Both, oft were feen in battles to engage ;

Oft fac'd grim death, when cloath'd in Gallic rage.

Ill fated warriors ! thus to fall before

Your lucklefs boat, had reach'd the deftin'd fhore !

Oh ! that you'd liv'd to tread the hoftile plain,

Till thoufands by your gallant Scotchmen flain,

Their furious blows had felt, and dropp'd around,

And you had fcap'd without your mortal wound !

Small caufe fhall Frenchmen have, your deaths to boaft,

When once your troops fhall firmly tread their coaft;

With angry courage fir'd, and gen'rous wrath,

They'll glut the grave, and fatiate greedy death !

As when the thunder of the mighty Jove,

Is hurl'd from heav'n's ftrong battlements above ;

The

The loud artill'ry in a dreadful form,

Comes rolling on, amid a pitchy ftorm ;

The direful fragors of th' Æthereal ftore,

Rattle aloft, with dread, terrific roar :

Lightnings, and bolts, before the growl proceed,

To ftrike the deftin'd mark, with rapid fury fpeed!

So under covert of fulphureous fmoke,

Which from the Britifh fleet in thunder broke ;

Firft flew the bolts, t' intimidate the Gauls,

To dafh the mud banks, or cemented walls.

Next Scotia's troops to battle fally'd forth,

And Louifbourg confefs'd their northern worth ;

From clouds of fmoke they burft like lightning's
        blaze,

And ftruck th' oppofing foe with grand amaze!

Few deaths they fent, of iron, or of lead,

But o'er the hoftile lines they boldly tread;

And as they march, they death and danger fpread.

To clofeft fight their cohort quickly runs,

And fcorns to battle with the diftant guns:

They ftrike the blow, that ftops the hoftile breath,

And load the foe with ftorms of fteely death!

See

See! where the fons of Scotland force their way,

With Rangers join'd, in dreadful difarray!

Suftain'd by infantry, array'd in order ftrong;

Amherft, and Wolfe, who urg'd the landing war

 along :

They fire, advance, and charge, and to the bat-

 tle throng.

And comet like, their broad bright fwords appear,

Death's in their front, and terror in their rear !

As fierce Achilles, (thunderbolt of war,)

Broke Trojan ranks in his refiftlefs carr;

On rufh'd his myrmidons, with faulchions rear'd,

Of troops thick throng'd, the ground was quickly

 clear'd.

So before, Wolfe and Amherft, Frenchmen fled,

Their troops advancing ftruck a mortal dread;

(The tim'rous living ftumbled o'er the dead!)

From flank, to flank, the glitt'ring danger fhines,

And war's dread havock, marks their fpreading lines;

They wave their fwords, anticipate the fight,

And ftrong reblaze the glitt'ring rays of light:

From man to man, they catch the gen'rous glow !

A ftupid languor feizes on the foe :

They ftand transfix'd! the burnifh'd ruin dread!

Thro' Gallia's troops a pannic terror fpread !

As when amid the gloom of darkeft night,

The tranfient glances of Tartarean light,

Attack a lonely perfon with furprize !

And fancy'd fiends in millions round him rife;

Mutely transfix'd, all refolution fleeps,

A chilly damp thro' all his vitals creeps;

A fweating tremor fhakes him to the ground,

Amid the tumult all reflection's drown'd.

So as their lines the Caledonians crofs'd,

The Frenchmen quick refifting ardour loft :

No longer felt the great heroic glow,

Such as the three united nations know :

Beneath their pond'rous blows, the French troops
    reel,

Deprefs'd, and drown'd, 'midft fhow'rs of northern
    fteel.

Our troops (refolv'd,) no dangers cou'd controul,

Tho' high on fhore, the foaming billows roll :

Tho'

Tho' thoufands there (entrench'd,) the beach command;

And guns, and mortars, throng'd the hoftile ftrand:

Headed by Wolfe, they plunge into the flood,

And wade to Louifbourg thro' Gallic blood!

Where Englifh, Scotch, and bold Hibernians ftorm,

How ftrong the triple union they can form!

The threefold pow'rs their gallantry difplay,

Like powder, fhot, and fire, impetuous force their way!

With circumfpection now the ground's furvey'd,

From whence artilleries may beft be play'd;

And heavy batt'ring guns are dragg'd around,

Advancing engineers work under ground:

Large and fmall batt'ries, (cover'd from the fight,)

Are plann'd, and form'd, midft filence of the night.

The platforms next, with utmoft fpeed they form,

From whence to roll Great Britain's thunder ftorm;

Incentive match, and bombs, are thither brought,

And magazines, with dormant thunder fraught;

Till wak'd by fire, then dafhing bolts are thrown,

To raze the walls of thick cemented ftone:

Mortars

Mortars are plac'd, from whofe infernal wombs,

Ejecting powder fends the murd'ring bombs.

Now every thing againft the hour prepar'd,

The mafks are dropp'd, the Britifh greeting's heard.

Towards the ramparts infantries advance,

Defiance thunders from the forts of France:

The loud explofion rages more and more,

Deep throated guns, and brazen mortars roar:

In undulating air, long hangs the found,

And flame, and fulph'rous vapours fpread around.

As from Mount Etna, and Vefuvius rife,

Thunders, and flames, whilft vapours cloud the fkies:

Like thefe vulcanoes in convulfive rage,

The Britifh troops, and Gallic forts engage.

Advancing corps of infantries gain ground,

The cohorn, fafcine batt'ries play around.

Wolfe well deferves his dread voracious name,

Spreads ruin round, or wide devouring flame !

Around the town he roams, conceal'd in night !

Intent on Gallic prey, maintains the fight !

The filenc'd light-houfe-batt'ry, owns his might !

Soon

Soon grows more dreadful, than it was before;

Infpir'd by Wolfe, and Britifh troops to roar!

Wolfe, on the ifland fort, his battle pours!

Inceffant, fends, his thund'ring, iron fhow'rs!

Whilft Amherft, on the town, and grand-fort plays!

(On Gallic troops, defponding terrors feize!)

Againft the ifland fort, Wolfe's bofom burns!

His rapid ftorm, their thunder overturns!

Dafh'd by his balls, obftruĉting ramparts drop!

They even plough, the deep foundations up!

Eefore his battle, adverfe ftrength is born!

Pomelions, nuts, and muzzles, off are torn!

His fierce affault, the hoftile platform feels,

Beftrew'd with ufelefs guns, and broken wheels!

The mould'ring breaches, wide, and wider fpread!

Rammers, and fponges, lie among the dead!

Defcending bombs, moft dreadfully difplode!

With ruin'd walls, the fhiver'd platforms load!

The fort's defendants, now for fhelter fly,

For undiftinguifh'd, lo, the rampiers lie!

Subverted guns, with wheels aloft difplay'd,

Among the piles of rubbifh, too are laid!

And dreadful devaftation widely fpread!

Difploded

Difploded fhells, and fhot, together throng;

And mortars, from their brazen bafes flung!

A profpect odd! of iron! brafs! and lead!

Of ftones! and mangled bodies of the dead!

Fathers, to future fons, fhall this report;

So, fought brave Wolfe! fo look'd, the ifland fort!

By Bofcawen, and Hardy, (both) infpir'd,

See, Britifh tars, to deeds of wonder fir'd!

They leave their lofty fhips upon the fea;

Deftin'd for Louifbourg, they fpeed their way,

As hungry wolves, will nightly roam for prey!

No whit difmay'd, thro' dangers on they came!

'Midft gloom, and fhot, and fhells, and fulph'rous
  flame!

Towards the Gallic thunder ftorms they bend!

With fpeed alert, their lofty fides afcend!

And from the engineers, the dafhing bolts they
  rend!

Defcending Frenchmen, foon their quarters leave,

The cutlafs, and the naval pole-ax, cleave!

         Not

Not one furvives, to wail the hundreds dead;

But carnage great, and total death is fpread!

L'Entreprenant, in flame, moft fiercely glow'd!

But Bienfaicant they fav'd, and from the harbour
        tow'd.

So hungry wolves, attack the tim'rous fheep,

In lonely cots, and o'er the fences leap;

Eager, they feize, upon the fleecy prey;

Tear! kill! and drag, whate'er they pleafe away!

With ardent balls, brave Wolfe, their fleet doth vex!

Or drops his bombs, upon their open decks!

They fink, or vanifh, in a fulph'rous blaze!

And with new horrors Louifbourg amaze!

As from the bellowing engine of the fkies,

The thunderbolt, and riving light'ning flies;

They rend the knotty oaks, and tear the ground!

And fpread a defolating ruin round!

So Wolfe, and Amherft, emulous advance,

To wafte the troops, and raze the forts of France!

                        Amherft,

Amherſt, ſends various deaths among the foe! ⎤
The troops, and tars, with gen'rous courage glow! ⎬
The town, and grand-fort, little reſpite know! ⎦

See, Wolfe, inſpires, and ſpurs his martial pow'rs!

With roar deſtructive, Louiſbourg devours!

Wolfe, prowls by night, with caution to ſurvey,

How batt'ring guns, and Britiſh mortars play!

Oft looks on Louiſbourg, with threat'ning frown!

And ſhow'rs his ſhot, and ſhells, upon the town!

Amherſt, and Wolfe, full forty days aſſail

The town, and forts, reſolved to prevail.

As oft are known, the meteors of the ſky,

With burning tails, deſcending from on high,

To daſh thro' houſes, quick in aſhes lain,

Tough oaks are riv'd, and frighted mortals ſlain:

As they diſplode, with dreadful thund'ring ſound,

And tear, and furrow up, the neighb'ring ground!

Their tow'ring bombs, deſcending from on high,

With dread commiſſion! to the town they fly!

The craſhing roofs give way! they daſh to ground!

Diſplode! and ſcatter duſt, and deaths, around!

Spread

Spread devaftation wide, thro' all the place!

And lofty domes, to deep foundations raze!

So, flaming Louifbourg, their fury feels!

From Englifh bombs, proceed thofe various ills!

Men! women! children! welter in their gore! ⎫
Shrieks! groans! and flames! mortars! and can- ⎬
      nons roar! ⎪
With dread confufion, fill the Gallic fhore! ⎭

Drucour, no longer, can the fight maintain;

Tho' greatly brave! yet here, his brav'ry's vain!

Tho' wond'rous ftrong the place, it cannot fhield

His troops from death; behold, the rampiers yield!

For Wolfe, and Amherft, with a thund'ring frown!

Shake the grand fort! and fire the neighb'ring town!

Aloft, great GEORGE's banners, were uprear'd;

Brave Bofcawen, into the harbour fteer'd.

The dreadful fcene is chang'd, they hear no more, ⎫
The dying groans, nor guns, nor mortars roar, ⎬
And flaughter, ceafes, on the Gallic fhore! ⎭

The Britifh cannon roar'd, in harmlefs fort,

When Louifbourg became a friendly port!

                               Heav'n!

Heav'n! hear my pray'r! preferve it as our own!

Till Gallic foes, our faithful friends are grown!

                          Amen.

WHEN Neftor, (fagely,) on the Phrygian fhore,

Advis'd fome * fpies, fhou'd Hector's camp explore,

The fage Ulyffes, and fierce Diomed,

Thro' Trojan guards, and gloom, and dangers fped.

Amherft, and Wolfe, like thefe, were wifely chofe,

For foreign war, againft perfidious foes.

* Upon the refufal of Achilles, to return to the army, (which he had deferted, on account of the quarrel between him, and Agamemnon, who with his troops had laid fiege to Troy; but was now by the irrefiftble prowefs of Hector, beaten back to his fhips, and entrenchments.) A council of war was call'd by night, for the public fafety, and Neftor queftions, if none will go to hazard his life to fave his country, ftrive to feize fome ftraggling foe, or penetrate fo far into their camp, as to hear their counfels and defigns, mentions the glory of the dead, and what gifts! and praifes! his grateful country wou'd beftow! Diomed, undertook this hazardous enterprize! and made choice of Ulyffes for his companion. In their paffage, they furprize Dolon (whom Hector had fent on a like defign, to the camp of the Grecians.) From him they are informed of the fituation of the Trojan, and auxiliary forces, and particularly of Rhefus, and the Thracians, who were lately arrived. They pafs on with fuccefs; kill Rhefus, with feveral of his officers, and feize the famous horfes of that prince, with which they return in triumph to the camp. The whole ftory may be read in the 10th book of Homer's Iliad.

                          Wifdom,

Wifdom, and valour, with united force ;

Conduct the Grecians, thro' their nightly courfe.

If fkill mature, the great defign fhou'd afk ;

Who fitter than Ulyffes, for the tafk ?

Shou'd giant danger, ftride a-crofs the path !

Tydides * fierce ! was full of martial wrath !

With mighty ftrength, his pond'rous fpear he drove !

And fcarce † retreated from the thund'ring Jove !

Amherft, in council, was rely'd upon :

Wolfe had the fpirit of Tydeus' fon !

Both oft had charg'd, amidft the fulph'rous roar

Of deep mouth'd guns, and thoufands in their gore:

Both oft well try'd, to fierce encounters drew,

Where iron deaths, and leaden dangers flew!

---

* Tydides, is Diomed, being the fon of Tydeus ; and is fometimes in the Iliad, call'd Diomed. Tydides. Tydeus's fon.

† In the 8th book of Homer's Iliad. We have Diomed. advancing fiercely to Neftor's refcue, and to battle with Hector, who came thund'ring through the war, and was driving full upon the Pylian fage. Homer makes Jupiter oppofe Diomed in thefe words.

> But Jove with awful found ;
> Roll'd the big thunder o'er the vaft profound.
> Full in Tydides' face, the lightning flew ;
> The ground before him, flam'd with fulphur blue.

After which, he defcribes him retreating with great reluctance, from Hector's overwhelming battle ; tho' deferted by the Grecians, advifed to flee by Neftor, and oppos'd by a ftorm of thunder, and lightning, from Jupiter himfelf.

Brunfwick,

Brunfwick, and Pitt, on thefe, fecurely lean'd,

England, in hope, by thefe, was well fuftain'd.

So Memnon, Neftor, fix'd their hopes upon

Bold Diomed, and fage Laertes' * fon.

Thro' Dardan ranks, victorious, both had ftrode;

Their Grecian fpears, drank, deep of hoftile blood.

Amidft the fierceft fhocks, both oft were try'd;

Whilft brains, and gore, their biting faulchions dy'd!

Swords, jav'lins, darts, and fpears, (in hoftile fields,)

In batt'ring ftorms, had rattled on their fhields!

With warlike fpoils, their labours oft were crown'd;

For wifdom great, and valour, much renown'd.

They feiz'd on Dolon †, ftruck with wild difmay !)

Firft flew the fpy, then fped where Rhefus lay :

Doom'd with his guards, no more to fee the light;

Their eyes feal'd up, in everlafting night !

Back to their friends, the heroes fafe return'd :

The Trojan camp, their nightly vifit mourn'd.

Both plann'd, both fought, as dread occafion needs !

And both their fouls, were form'd for mighty deeds !

* Ulyffes, who is in the Iliad, fometimes call'd, fage Ulyffes,
wife Ulyffes, Laertes's fon, and fometimes Ithacus.
† The fpy, fent by Hector, to explore the Grecian Camp.
Vid. 10th book of Homer's Iliad.

Amherft,

Amherſt, and Wolfe, like theſe, in war renown'd!

Return'd from Louiſbourg, with conqueſt crown'd!

The toils of war, each diſpoſition ſuits;

And either plans, and either executes.

The Grecian heroes, their nocturnal courſe

Held jointly on, with great united force.

Whilſt Diomed, the guards of Rheſus ſlew,

Wiſe Ithacus *, the bodies backward drew.

Fearing the mettled ſteeds might ſcorn the rein,

Unus'd to carnage, and the ſanguin'd plain.

Whilſt Amherſt thunder'd on the frighten'd town!

Wolfe's battle ſhook the iſland battr'y down!

Wiſe were the Grecian chiefs! nor wont to fear!

Sagacious! brave! the Britiſh heroes were!

***

* Ulyſſes, who is often call'd Ithacus: from his country; being king of Ithaca.

End of B O O K I.

The

The ARGUMENT.

The defcent at Cherburg. Blowing up the bafon. Goree attacked by the Honourable Auguftus Keppel: and furrendered to him. Admiral Rodney's bombardment of Havre de Grace; and burning the flatbottom boats; with an addrefs to Great Britain. Bofcawen's failing, and chafing De Clue. The engagement. De Clue, and part of his fquadron, driven on fhore! with the pannic they were in on feeing the Spanifh fleet, and fuppofing them to be an Englifh fleet.

WAR:

W A R:

B O O K II.

GREAT GEORGE's GRANDSON, lands on Gallia's fhore!

His batt'ring guns! and royal mortars roar!

Clofe ply'd, well aim'd, are bombs, and dafhing balls!

Before the princely hero, Cherburg falls!

Low as the duft, ftrong ramparts, down are thrown!

Aloft, in air, the coftly bafon's blown!

How fmil'd, our good, old King! how trembled Gaul!

Whilft EDWARD's cannon, raz'd proud Cherburg's wall!

Paternal doubts! and ardent wifhes rife!

Whilft tears of tranfport, fparkled in his eyes!

D 2   Grandly

Grandly exulting! more than king he ftood-!

Whilft EDWARD fought, confeffing Brunfwick's
blood!

So ftands, the royal hunter, to furvey

His cubs, who grapple with a ftubborn prey!

He fwings his tail, exulting at the fight!

And trembling, longs to mingle in the fight!

With love paternal fir'd, and ardent rage!

He fees the lions, as the cubs engage!

At length, the vanquifh'd foe, is drown'd in blood!

He fhakes his mane, and roars his approbation
loud!

As if Vefuvius, uprooted torn;

Againft Goree, to battle had been born!

Brave Keppel, in the Torbay, fierce affail'd,

Fort, after fort, and mightily prevail'd!

Whilft fate, in triumph, in each broadfide rode,

Troops, tars, and Keppel, all, for vict'ry glow'd!

Shot, after fhot, bomb, after bomb, he fent!

Silenc'd their guns! platforms, and ramparts rent!

The Gauls grew cold, as warm the Britons grew!

And greatly emulous, to battle flew!

They ceas'd their fire, and pull'd their enfign down,

And gave our troops poffeffion of the town.

See! Rodney, next, th' invafive project marr!

Subverts French fchemes, and their flat bottom'd war!

Britannia's fleet, at Havre, threats the fhore!

And brazen mortars, in bombardment roar!

From iron vehicles, the veng'ance broke!

And all their plans, evaporate in fmoke!

Britain! let loofe thy rough, undaunted tars!

And fmile applaufe, on all thy fons of Mars!

Let no cabals, thy patriots aims fruftrate!

Nor civil difcontent, difturb the ftate!

Then under Providence, we may expect,

A lafting peace, the pride of Gallia checkt!

Now

Now Hawke, and Bofcawen, with terrors ride,

Acrofs the main, to curb the Gallic pride :

And in Lagos, and Quiberon's fam'd bay,

Our gallant tars, their naval worth difplay ;

Attack, and ftrike the fleets of Gaul, with dread

    difmay !

Bofcawen, firft engages with the foe ;

And gains new laurels from his overthrow!

Frighted before! at Spaniards * in the bay ;

They tack'd, confus'd ! and ftood again at fea.

Chimeras fill'd their minds! black fear prevails !

And ev'ry cloud, was England's fwelling fails !

So tim'rous fouls, (dreading nocturnal fhade !)

A fimilar miftake, have often made.

A fudden glance, a-crofs a glitt'ring pool,

'Twas light'ning flafh'd ! and fhou'd fome growling

    bull,

Bellow terrific, thro' th' adjacent plains,

Some fiend infernal, roar'd, and fhook his chains!

---

* The French fleet, feeing the Spanifh fleet in the bay, (as
they were going into harbour,) tack'd, and ftood off again at
fea : by which means, they met, the (fo much dreaded) Englifh
fleet, which they fo vainly endeavoured to fhun.

From

From non-exifting ills, they ftrive t' efcape,

Stumble on nought ! and into ditches leap!

So Frenchmen now, fubftantial dangers meet,

Shunning the fhadow of an Englifh fleet !

Our fleet, no fooner, to their view appear'd,

Falfe fignals made, and Britain's enfigns rear'd,

Thro' all their fhips, the wonted fears prevail!

They dropp'd their (courfers, and fet ev'ry fail!

Now glow'd our tars ! and thro' the foaming fea,

They chas'd De Clue, and long'd to feize their prey!

As thro' the concave of the gloomy fky,

(On wings of winds upborn, on which they fly ;)

Black clouds, chafe clouds, in dread tremendous

       form !

Pregnant with light'ning, hail, and thunder ftorm!

So Gallia's flying fhips, and our purfuing fleet,

Glide on in flaming gloom, and in loud thunder

      greet !

Yard-arm, and yard-arm now, and fide, to fide,

Pikes, piftols, guns, and cannons all are ply'd.

From fhip, to fhip, grapples, and chains are thrown ;

Pole axes grafp'd, and cutlaffes are drawn :

With

With inborn glow, our tars prepare t' affail,

Refolv'd they board, and uncontroul'd prevail.

Braye Bofcawen bears down, with gen'rous rage;

And tho' difmafted, dares De Clue t' engage.

So fierce they fought! fo many broadfides fir'd!

The brafs * relented, and the guns grew tir'd!

De Clue now fled, (with thoufands) hid in fmoke,

Which from the Britifh fleet, with veng'ance
      broke;

And left their fhips, at random on the fea,

To rocks, and flames, and Englifh tars a prey.

To fhun Bofcawen's rage, and horrid roar,

The Gallic Ocean † tumbled on the fhore.

* If I am not much miftaken, I heard, that the muzzles, of fome of the Ocean's brafs guns, bent downward; the metal being molify'd, by exceffive heat of the oft repeated difcharges.
† The fhip De Clue commanded.

End of BOOK II.

The

Great Britain's *preparation of her fleet, and troops,*
against Quebec, under Admiral Saunders, and Ad-
miral Holmes; and the Generals, Wolfe, Monckton,
and Townshend. The pannic in France! and at
Quebec! as the consequence thereof. The fleet fail-
ing; their arrival in the river of Quebec. The
formidable appearance, and resolution, of the Eng-
lish, Scotch, Irish, and Provincials; when they re-
member'd Zell, and the scalping butchery of the
French, Canadians, and Indians. The fleet pro-
ceeding up the Gulf, and the English Wolfe landed
against the enemy. His intrepidity, and the execu-
tion of his attacks. Fireships sent down, several
times by the French, upon the stream, to burn our
fleet; but by the vigilance of Admiral Saunders,
Holmes, and other resolved commanders; join'd with
the indefatigable resolution, and activity, of our
bold, and hardy tars; they are baffled in all their
schemes, and the fireships, and fire-floats, do no da-
mage to the English fleet. The vexation of the French
thereon; and the war carried to their walls. The
united battery of General Wolfe, on Point Levi:
Admiral Saunders, below the town, and Admiral
Holmes, above the town.

General *Wolfe, represented as in suspense, on point*
of Levi; on account of the small number of forces
he had with him, and on viewing Montcalm's camp,

with

with near double the number ; and obferving the ftu-
pendous height, and ftability of the town, and gar-
rifon of Quebec. Compared to Babylon's, (as was
thought, impregnable) ramparts, for the town ftood
upon a lofty rock, and well defended by trênch, on
trench, and impaffable works, and avenues : rifing
dreadfully to view! one above another. General
Wolfe's intrepid refolves, to attack Monfieur Mont-
calm's entrenchments. The dangerous landing : fight,
and retreat. The undaunted behaviour of Captain
Ochterlony, (a Scotch gentleman,) and Lieut. Pey-
ton, (an Irifh gentleman :) both of one company of
Royal American grenadiers ; left wounded on the
field of battle. Their refufal to be carried off. Two
Indians, and a Frenchman, attack Capt. Ochterlony.
Mr. Peyton, (after a long ftruggle,) kills the In-
dians, and is refcu'd from about thirty more by three
Highlanders, detached by Capt. M‘Donald of Fra-
fer's battalion. General Wolfe is vex'd at his re-
pulfe, and fickens thro' care and watching. The
united efforts of the foldiers, and feamen, to reduce
the place. The battery againft, and from the town,
and all the terrors! carnage! and tumult of the
fiege defcrib'd! the terror of the French, Canadians,
and Indians, on account of their cruelty, and trea-
chery!

General Amherft, Townfhend, Johnfon, Howe, Pri-
deaux, Rogers, Forbes, Schomberg, Abercromby,
and

and their transactions on the Continent mentioned, by way of episode; who reduced in the mean time, Ti-conderoga, Crown Point, and Niagara; with some other services performed by them. The siege of Quebec reassumed. The day of battle describ'd before the town. The difficulty our troops met in ascending the hill, and their resolution. The summit of the hill gain'd. The armies meeting. A short essay on the Generals. The fight begun. General Wolfe's wrist broken by a ball. His intrepidity, and desire for battle. General Wolfe wounded a second time; but dissembles the hurt. Wounded a third time, mortally! drops, and is carried out of the battle. The manner of his death! and how it was received at home. His mother's grief, and England's in general. The generosity of the common people, at the time of rejoicing and illumination. A short address to his mother. The grief of the soldiers in the battle for him. Their generous rage! impetuous! and overwhelming united attack of the enemy! Colonel Howe's station in the field.

A description of the Anstruthers and Scots, with their broad swords, and the rest of the troops, with their bayonets fix'd; piercing thro', hewing down whole lanes of carnage! and rolling the Gallic squadrons before them, in confusion! General Monckton wounded: his behaviour, and a short parallel between him and General Townshend.

General

General Townſhend takes the command. His addreſs, ſkill, and intrepidity; like Achilles, leading on his myrmidons to battle, to revenge the death of his dear Patroclus! the wounded Ulyſſes! Diomed! &c. &c. &c. The general rout, and ſlaughter of Montcalm and his troops. Bougainville's corps appears, juſt as the rout began: but are ſoon likewiſe routed by General Townſhend, and our animated troops, and ſent full ſpeed, to join the reſt in their retreat.

The chaſe continued to the town of Quebec: our troops mixing with, running down, and taking the French-men priſoners at will, with the ſurrender of the town and garriſon, to General Townſhend.

WAR:

W A R:

B O O K III.

CHERBURG, Du Quefne, Goree, and
Senegal;
Victims, to Britain's fierce refentment
fall!

The like black fate, did Guadaloup betide!
Strong Louifbourg we made our own befide:
The Gallic, captiv'd fleets, in Britifh harbours ride!
Lewis no caufe has got, whereof to boaft;
Nor Royal GEORGE to grieve, that he Minorca loft:
How fatiate now, Great Britain might fit down!
But Brunfwick, ftill puts on a threat'ning frown!
By Pitt, (refolv'd to awe the wond'ring world!)
Againft Quebec, the Englifh thunder's hurl'd!

With

With mifchief fure, the bolts deftructive fly !
Guided by Him, who thunders from the fky !
From Pole, to Pole, great Albion's terror's known ! ⎫
She roars in thunder ! and her pow'r they own, ⎬
Amid the frigid and the torrid Zone ! ⎭

Winter elaps'd, the welcome fpring appears ;
Saunders, aloft, the Britifh enfign rears !
Englifh, Hibernians, Scotchmen, all combine; ⎫
With one confent, (refolv'd,) united join, ⎬
T'imbark, and boldly urge the grand defign ! ⎭
Tents, horfes, carrs, are in great plenty fhipt !
And hardy troops, for wafting war equipt !
For cannonading, 'gainft the Gallic forts ;
They've pond'rous guns, and fhot of various forts.
Fufes, and fhells, by thoufands now they get,
And brazen mortars, for bombardment fit.
Cargoes are fhipt, of black, infernal grain !
T'eject the balls, in thunder, on the main :
With large referves, from Britain's ordnance ftore,
For field artill'ries, on the Gallic fhore.

Incentive

Incentive match, is put on board the fleet,

And all the tools, for pioneering meet.

The gath'ring ſhips, from various harbours glide,

And at one gen'ral rendezvous they ride.

The Grecian fleet, ſo met, for Trojan doom;

When Paris raviſh'd Helen from her home.

So glow'd the troops, to raze proud Illium's walls,

Only they wanted powder, bombs, and balls!

Commiſſion'd now, brave Adm'ral Saunders ſails,

At Paris, ſad foreboding fear, prevails!

The coaſt of France, a pannic dread alarms!

Britannia's angry ſons, are rous'd again to arms!

As when a flock of ſwans have ken'd on high,

A dreaded eagle, ſouſing from the ſky!

They flutter, ſcream, and gather cloſely round,

And wiſh, a place of ſafety could be found!

Till down he comes, upon the pinion'd prey;

Scatters, and tears, and bears a ſwan away!

When Saunders ſail'd, in France ſuch moan was
        heard;

But Quebec, chiefly, his approaches fear'd!

There

There Alb'on's, thunders, did most fiercely roar! ⎫
Quebec, (well mann'd!) from Lewis, reeking tore! ⎬
And laid Canadians, welt'ring in their gore! ⎭
So oft, before, have England's Adm'rals hurl'd,
Great GEORGE's flame, and terror, thro' the world!

Wide o'er the deep, thro' storms, and blust'ring gales,
Safe to America, our squadron sails.
Provincials there, against Quebec defign'd,
And, friendly ships, with Saunders are combin'd.
Provincials, English, Scotch, Hibernians bold!
Frown, formidably, dreadful to behold!
Canadian scalping now, before their eyes, ⎫
And butcher'd fathers, mothers, wives, and chil- ⎬
    dren rife! ⎭
And ev'ry cruel treach'ry, which the Gauls devise!
Gloomy they low'r, like pond'rous show'rs, when
    born,
Towards a field, of yellow standing corn.
Till down a deluge comes, with rattling found,
And beats the plenteous harvest to the ground;

So

So Britain's troops, when they remember'd Zell,*
And fcalping knives, frown'd with refentment fell,
With gen'rous rage! they beat Quebec to ground!
And recompence moft juft, the black Canadians
    found.

Saunders proceeds up thro' St. Laurence gulf;
And fends, (to prowl) on fhore, the Englifh Wolfe!
Who with an (eager,) martial tranfport flew,
Upon the black, Canadian, fcalping crew!
Yet warm from Louifbourg, and blood of Gaul!
He long'd to fee the favage fcalpers fall.
Keen threat'ning fires, he fhot from wrathful eyes,
Whilft from his brazen engines, veng'ance flies.
His manly bofom burn'd, with freeborn flame!
To fpread the terror of his fov'reign's name.
He burft like fate, againft the Indian foe;
And whelm'd them in the Gallic overthrow!

   * The place in Germany, where Monfieur Richlieu, burnt
the Orphan Houfe, and fo many hundred orphans in it.

E   To

To vex the foe, (whom num'rous forts immure,)
And Britain's fleet from danger to secure,
Levi at firſt, and Orleans they poſſeſs'd ;
And to the batt'ring ſiege, themſelves addreſs'd.
Our troops urg'd on, drove Gauls, and Indians back,
Reſolv'd with ſpeed, the caſtle to attack.
As mortal palſies, e'er they ſeize the heart,
Attack, and weaken, man's extremeſt part :
At length, death urges on the fatal ſtrife,
Surrounds the breaſt, attacks the ſeat of life ;
So Wolfe devour'd the interjacent ground ;
Reſolv'd advanc'd, and ſcatter'd terrors round !

Large, and ſmall faſcine batt'ries, ſoon are plann'd ;
And guns, and murd'ring mortars, quickly mann'd !
Great ſtore of ſhells, and ſhot, and black diſplod-
    ing grain,
Are ſent on ſhore, to Wolfe, nor are they ſent in
    vain ;
He deals with martial wrath, deſtruction thro'
    the plain !

Whilſt

Whilſt Wolfe, and Saunders, 'gainſt Quebec com-
    bine,

The French (alarm'd,) had plann'd a dire deſign,

To execute a dreadful fiery * doom!

And in relentleſs blaze, the fleet conſume.

As Etna oft, with ſulph'rous flame, and noiſe,

Subjacent towns, and cities, quick deſtroys ;

Whene'er inrag'd, the mountain overflows,

And from its womb, th' infernal mixture throws :

So from Quebec, (adrift,) the Gallic flame ;

Down thro' the Gulf, againſt brave Saunders came!

Toward the Britiſh fleet, the floating terrors ride,

In awful manner born, upon the rapid tide ;

The thronging, blazing deaths, a little fleet appear!

Involv'd in pitchy gloom! and cloath'd around

    with fear!

As if th' infernal coaſt, (itſelf,) was drawing near!

---

* Whilſt Gen. Wolfe, and Admiral Saunders, were uniting
their utmoſt efforts, to batter, deſtroy, and take the town: or
bring Monſ. de Montcalm, (an able fortunate and brave commander) to battle : the French ſeveral times ſent down from the
town, on the rapid ſtream, fireſhips, and boats, full of com-
buſtibles, to deſtroy our ſhipping, which almoſt wholly filled
the channel. But by the extraordinary ſkill, and vigilance of
Admiral Saunders ; the bravery, and intrepidity of his officers,
and ſailors, every veſſel of this kind ſent againſt them, was
tow'd aſhore, without doing the leaſt miſchief.

Saunders

Saunders aware, defcry'd 'em from afar,

- And foon prepar'd to meet the flaming war!

Great Britain's tars, toward the danger fpeed!

And prov'd they were, true Englifhmen indeed!

For as the Grecians gather'd from a far,

When Hector urg'd along the flaming war,

Round Ajax throng'd, his near approach to greet,

To fell their lives, and fave the Grecian fleet.

(Begirt with Trojans *, on the hero came!

And high uplifted, bore, the Phrygian flame!)

Refolv'd they fix'd, nor ever once gave ground,

Till Hector's flame, in Trojan blood was drown'd!

So Englifh failors, glow'd with fierce defires,

Refolv'd to quell, thofe num'rous floating fires!

* The whole ftory, of the battle near the fhip of the dead
Protefilaus; the compact body, and immoveable refolution, of
the Grecian Phalanx, around the two Ajaces, and feveral other
commanders, oppofing the defperate, and formidable onfet of
Hector; (exulting in his having paffed the wall, which guarded
the fhips, and the Grecian camp;) begirt with the fierceft, and
prime warriors of his army, and the numerous bands of the
then triumphant Trojans, rufhing furioufly on after, (like a deluge,) with the fiery war: the Grecians ftruggles to repulfe the
Trojans, and fave the fleet; and the Trojans' efforts, to rufh
on, and burn the fleet, with the fcale of battle turn'd, by
the approach of Patroclus, in Achilles's armour, and chariot,
with Hector's retreat, the Grecian navy fav'd, from Hector's
flame, the Trojan rout, and carnage, which enfu'd; may be
read in the fifteenth, and fixteenth books of Homer's Iliad.

Boats,

Boats, throng on boats, as near the firefhips drew!

Clap'd clofe on board, and chains, and grapples
     threw!

With bufy, anxious minds, they boldly wrought!

And Gallia's burning fcheme, reduc'd to nought!

Canadians, Gauls, fruftrated, all in vain,

Gnafhing their teeth, to fenfelefs walls complain,

Juft as a hungry wolf, but flowly flies,

Whilft dogs, and fhepherds, follow with their cries,

Grinning, oft turns, with fear, and fierce difdain,

Reluctant runs, and quits the bleating plain,

His favage fiercenefs, fcarcely can with-hold,

So grinn'd Quebec, by providence controul'd!

So fled their tars, when our brave tars appear'd!

They heard their fhouts, their boift'rous greeting
     fear'd.

Tho' fev'ral fhips, with fires infernal glow'd! ⎫

From larboard, ftarboard clear, each flame was ⎬

     tow'd!

Whilft Brunfwick's fhips, at anchor fafely rode. ⎭

Britain

Britain exult! to wond'ring nations tell,

Thy tars, wou'd grapple with a floating hell!

Thus oft, the French fent down their horrid fires,

As oft our, failors glow'd with fierce defires,

To grapple with the flaming fulph'rous war!

T'oppofe their boats! and all their fchemes to mar!

Where flame, and death, and war, tumultous rage!

There fhout the Britifh tars! and with delight engage!

As Grecians turn'd the burning war to Troy,

And did that long defended town deftroy,

Saunders, and Wolfe, and Holmes, repay'd the
  Gauls ;

And brought Great Britain's thunder to their walls.

From Levi's Point, Wolfe's rapid ftorm came down!

Saunders below, and Holmes above the town,

(Intent on war, in fulminating fort,)

Eject their bolts, to raze the Gallic fort.

         From

From ships, and batt'ries, (with deftruction ftor'd)

In triple concert, England's veng'ance roar'd.

On Levi's Point, Wolfe ruminating ftood;

Thence Montcalm's camp, and ftrong Quebec he
    view'd.

Quebec! whofe bafe, was on a lofty rock!

Difpos'd to ftand, amidft the fierceft fhock!

Tho' Englifh fleets, the garrifon furround!

And Englifh armies, throng th' adjacent ground!

Like thofe, on Babylon's ftupendous wall! *

Who fear'd no foes, tho' heav'n fhou'd threat the fall!

By art, and nature form'd, for ftrong defence!

With proud difdain! the French look'd down from
    thence.

* The people of Babylon, when the city was befieg'd, look'd
down with a fearlefs difdain, on the troops which beleaguer'd
the walls, and trufted to their ftupendous height, and ftrength.
So Quebec, both by art and nature, was moft ftrongly fortify'd,
and render'd capable of an obftinate defence.

On

On glorious death, or well earn'd conqueſt bent:

Wolfe, with his troops, to Montmorenci * went:

Attack'd the trenches, brav'd the num'rous foe!

Who ſculk'd behind their banks, and fear'd an
overthrow.

The time deciſive now, come on to ſtorm,

And death put on, a fierce, tremendous form!

His vanguard, were the terrors of the night!

Wolfe, Monckton, Townſhend, whetted for the
fight!

Engliſh, Hibernians, Caledonians, arm'd

With native rage, for dang'rous battle warm'd!

Provincials too, with emulation came!

And march'd intrepid, to the field of fame,

And Britiſh tars, as ſtrong reſerves await;

To join the chace, or favour the retreat,

* The place, near where Monſ. Montcalm was entrench'd.

Inviron'd

Inviron'd thus; midft terrors on he came !

With Britain's thunderbolts, and fulph'rous flame!

Now near the fhore, th' affailing forces drew,

And leaden deaths, (like hail,) in volleys flew.

Englifh, Canadians, French, drop all around;

Guns, men, and blood, beftrew the flipp'ry ground.

French deep-mouth'd guns, difgorge their murd'r-
      ing glut !

From front to rear, wide lanes of carnage cut!

Defcending bombs, (from num'rous forts of Gaul,)

Among the troops, and boats, in plenty fall !

Promifcuous kill! with fulminating light,

Difplode, and add, new terrors to the fight !

The troops, and tars, rufh'd on, with martial wrath !

Thro' floods of flame ! and deluges of death !

Wolfe, and his men, thro' dangers, fpeed to fhore!

Where Gallic guns, and murd'ring mortars roar!

Gauls, and Canadians, mix'd, engage ten deep !

Our troops attempt, an afcent, rough, and fteep !

And

And on the neck of danger, dare to land!

Where Gallia's thick mud banks, were ten times
mann'd! .

At length retreat; (for numbers gain'd the day,)

Whilft Peyton *, 'mongft the dead, and wounded
lay.

Not far: (defcending to the fhades of night;)

Lay Ochterlony †, in a difmal plight!

Their two great hearts, by martial glow were fir'd!

And both their fouls, fweet friendfhip's flame infpir'd!

Of characters unblam'd! and free from ftains!

Link'd firm as fate, in amicable chains!

The grenadiers, wou'd fain their help beftow;

And bear them (wounded,) from the fcene of woe!

No gen'rous friends! the Caledonian faid!

Bear that brave man, (in fafety,) from the dead!

Pointing to Peyton, with his fractur'd bene:

Here let me lie, and bleed to death alone.

---

* Mr. Peyton, was an Irifh gentleman, Lieut. of Capt. Ochterlony's company of grenadiers.

† Mr. Ochterlony, was a Scotch gentleman, and captain of
a company of Royal American grenadiers. He, and Mr. Peyton, were infeparable friends, and of unblemifh'd characters.

Peyton

Peyton refus'd, with generous difdain !

To leave his friend, upon the hoftile plain !

Fierce as the dragon, guards th' Hefperian fruit,

Lay bleeding, (warm'd) to meet the dread difpute!

Here feems for death, an emulating ftrife,

Peyton fome minutes, guards departing life ;

And Ochterlony, with his dying breath,

Begs Peyton's refcue, from the field of death !

As there they lay among the num'rous flain,

Two fcalping murderers, (with cruel mein,)

Join'd by a Gaul, towards the warriors drew ;

And acted like a plund'ring * highway crew.

Now Ochterlony rofe, from off the ground :

(Tho' pain'd, and bleeding, from a mortal † wound!)

* They took Mr. Peyton's laced hat from him, and robbed
Capt. Ochterlony of his watch, and money, then one of the
Indians, attempted to knock his brains out, with his firelock,
and the other difcharged into his body, and ftabbed him with
his fcalping knife.

† He was fhot thro' the lungs, with a mufket ball: wore no
fword in the action, and was obliged to drop his fufee, long
before ; fo that now, he was quite unarm'd.

Within

Within his reach, no friendly weapon faw,

Wherewith to deal, the Caledonian blow!

Elfe, doubtlefs, all, his mighty blows had felt!

And fall'n beneath the ftrokes, his rage had dealt!

As dying lions, wide deftruction fpread!

Crufh dogs, and men! and fink, together, dead!

With firelock's clubb'd, they fought to lay him low,

And on his fhoulder *, laid the pond'rous blow!

Another, full of favage, (Gallic) wrath!

Pour'd in his breaft, a load * of leaden death!   .

Not fatiate yet, a third effort he made ;

And thro' his belly, plung'd his fcalping * blade!

Moft fiercely kneeling †, midft his murd'ring foes,

His naked hands, ftill parry'd off their blows!

He call'd to wounded Peyton, deeply pain'd ;

And of the outrage, to his friend complain'd ‡.

*** One of the Indians, attempted to knock him on the head, miffed the blow, and laid it on his fhoulder; the other difcharged into his breaft, and ftabbed him in the belly with his fcalping knife. He ftill ftood, and call'd to Mr. Peyton, O Peyton! the villain has fhot me!

† They brought him on his knees, by repeated blows and efforts, and thought to ftrangle him with his fafh : but he, ftill (tho' fo often and deadly wounded,) with furprifing exertion, baffled them : and after all, got into the town, lived fome days, and died there.

‡ He cried out, O Peyton! the villain has fhot me!

As

'As rufh'd the Trojan hero*, from the fhade,

And dealt deftruction, with his mortal blade !

Soon as he faw, (the fatal,) yawning wound !

And a brave dying friend, upon the ground!

Like him, fierce Peyton, ftraightway, boldly rear'd!

Defiance frown'd ! and both the Indians dar'd !

Rouz'd, tho' in pain! 'twixt bravery, and hate !

He groan'd in † flame ! and fent the leaden fate !

Which gain'd th' event, the gallant Peyton hop'd,

By death arrefted, down an Indian dropp'd !

On Ochterlony fell, (defign'd his prey !)

And grinning, groan'd his favage foul away !

When Furio faw his mate, bereav'd of life,

Frowning he grafp'd, his fatal, fcalping knife !

Fiercely, toward the wounded Peyton fped !

In fancy feiz'd his fcalp, and doom'd him dead !

The bold Hibernian, ftill unconquer'd ftood !

His fractur'd leg, pour'd out the vital blood !

* Nifus, who with Uryalus, iffued from Eneas's camp, flew Rhamnes, Rhemus, and many others, of the enemy's camp, and marched onward, to warn Eneas of their danger: but were met by Volfcens, in the wood, with 300 horfe, two of which, befides Volfcens, Nifus flew, in revenge of the gallant Uryalus, flain by them.

† Mr. Peyton had a double barrell'd fufee.

Tho'

Tho' his firm heart, of blood, was nearly dráin'd!

Refenting rage, and courage, yet remain'd!

Tho' wounded, left, upon the hoftile field!

To Indian foes, he greatly fcorn'd to yield!

For as the favage, nearer to him drew,

His fcorn encreas'd, and refolution grew!

On one foot poiz'd again, he boldly fir'd:

But fate deny'd, the great event defir'd!

The Indian's breaft, receiv'd the miffive ball: ⎫

But ftill, unfhock'd, as if it ftruck a wall; ⎬

He fhew'd no fign of pain, and fcorn'd to fall! ⎭

'Gainft Peyton, he, the leaden ruin fent:

Which ah! full fure, the hero's fhoulder rent!

Then onward rufh'd, full of Canadian pride!

His bay'net flefh'd, and thruft it thro' his fide.

The fecond thruft, he found himfelf deceiv'd;

Peyton's left hand, the fanguin'd point receiv'd;

Which feiz'd the mufket, with uncommon wrath!

Whilft his right hand, drew forth the glitt'ring *

    death.

He play'd again, the brave Hibernian's part;

And plung'd his faithful dagger to his heart!

* Mr. Peyton, luckily wore a dagger.

Now

Now hand, to hand, they join, and face, to face!
And grafp, and ftruggle, in a clofe embrace!
For prey, the Indian, ftill maintain'd the ftrife :
Peyton, for vict'ry fought, for fame, and life!
He oft his dagger plung'd, and groan'd, and frown'd,
And fpurn'd th' infernal fcalper to the ground!

So wounded tygers, on Eaft Indian plains,
Run down by blacks, and vex'd with pungent pains;
Drop to the ground, and feem to pant for breath,
A prey, almoft, to grim, all conq'ring death :
But on th' approach, of black purfuing foes,
Again reviv'd, their innate courage glows :
Rampant, they rear, and roar, and fwing their tails;
With deadly fangs, and lacerating nails ;
They tear, and kill, and ftain the place with blood!
Walk growling off! and fhelter in the wood !
As Peyton limp'd, with cruciating pain,
After he had Canadian fcalpers flain.

A

A band * of favage Indians, now drew near:

But Peyton fac'd, as if forgot to fear.

As if grim death, had brandifh'd high his dart;

They ftood aloof, and terror fill'd each heart!

So Ajax turn'd and frown'd at Illium's tow'rs;

When Grecians fled, from conq'ring Trojan pow'rs;

A living bulwark, in the rear remain'd;

The chafe retarded, and the charge fuftain'd!

The mean foul'd French, feem'd on his death intent;

And from the breaftwork, thund'ring volleys fent.

Peyton, (as if, invulnerable,) ftood,

Sedate in pain, their grov'ling rancour view'd.

For Mighty Fate, fruftrated fpightful Gauls;

To right, and left, wide flew the hiffing balls!

As he fuch wonders, in their fight had done!

So bravely fought! and dear bought vict'ry won!

* Thefe were a company of above 30, in full march, to deftroy him: but when he fac'd about, the foremoft halted, and
waited to be join'd by their fellows, but he kept them all at a
diftance, till three brave Highlanders, (detached from a fmall
party, headed by Capt. Macdonald, a Scotch gentleman,) came
to his timely refcue, and carried him off the field of battle.

French

French harmlefs cannon, took a random aim!

They roar'd applaufe! and thunder'd loud acclaim!

Macdonald * now, (with emulating flame,)

Amid furrounding dangers, fiercely came:

And with his little party, rufh'd'along,

Before him, French and Indians, fearful throng.

As bears, when chas'd, will fometimes make a ftand,

And rufh triumphant, thro' the hunting band;

For ftolen cubs, with double fury burn!

And fcatter death, which way foe'er they turn!

So for his fall'n friend, Macdonald ftray'd,

And bore him from the field of battle dead.

As round he turn'd, his anxious bufy fight,

He faw brave Peyton, in diftreffed plight:

Sent three fierce Highlanders, acrofs the field;

Who from the favages, the hero fhield.

* Mr. Macdonald was a Scotch gentleman, a captain in Col.
Frazer's battalion, who came for a young gentleman his ki, f-
man, who dropped on the field of battle, and bore him in
triumph off, againft all oppofition.

F   'Midft

'Midſt volleys*, flame *, and deaths*, and Gallic*

    fire;

With him, (triumphant,) from the foes retire!

Like Scipio†, thro' the field, with carnage ſtrow'd;

So he, upon the Scotchman's ſhoulders rode!

Now providence once more, eſpous'd their cauſe;

Again, French cannon, harmleſs roar'd applauſe!

Here brightly-ſhines, another glorious ſtrife,

Th' Hibernian ‡ ſav'd the Caledonian's ‡ life:

And now Macdonald, thirſting after fame,

(From Indian knives,) to Peyton's reſcue came.

**** They were about 60 yards from the enemy's breaſt-work, and troops, who kept a continual fire of cannon, and ſmall arms, on him and them, but they got all triumphant off.

† Young Scipio, took his father on his ſhoulders, when in danger, and carried him thro' the enemy's battle, to a place of ſafety. It may be read in the Carthaginian war.

‡‡ Mr. Peyton at firſt, killed the Indians attempting to kill Capt. Ochterlony; and now Mr. Macdonald, a Scotch Captain, reſcues Mr. Peyton from a party of Indians coming down upon him: the whole ſtory may be read at large, in the Britiſh Magazine of January, 1760.

                               Repuls'd,

Repuls'd, and vex'd, uncertain of fupplies;
Wolfe view'd the lofty town, with ardent eyes !
And whilft he plann'd the methods to prevail,
(Refolv'd he wou'd the garrifon affail;)
His mighty foul, within his bofom rag'd,
And war inteftine, with his body wag'd.
His enterprizing mind, by glory fir'd !
To honour's fummit, emulous afpir'd !
His genius active ! but his body flow !
To counteract, the ftrong, the Gallic foe !
As guns are worn, by fierce expanding flame ;
Refolves intrepid, fhook his tender frame !

Tho' firft, the landing in difpute was held,
And Britain's troops by numbers were repell'd ;
Like hungry lions, (foaming for their prey;)
Our troops again prepare to force their way.
As ev'ry grain, with joint impulfive force,
The bullet urges, in its rapid courfe;

Soldiers,

Soldiers *, and failors *, join'd againſt the Gauls,

With bombs, and bullets, raz'd the hoſtile walls.

French, and Canadians, under covert get ;

Death glances ſwift, along the parapet.

Rais'd up aloft, deſcending death comes down,

Like Egypt's hail, upon the ſubjeƈt town !

Which mix'd with fierce æthereal flame around,

Beat man, and beaſt, and cattle to the ground !

So glancing bombs, dance madly thro' the ſtreet:

And with diſploſion fierce, their houſes greet :

Which piece-meal torn, to open view diſplay'd,

The baſes of the ſtrongeſt domes are laid !

Men, women, children, midſt the flame are loſt !

To atoms rent ! and into nothing toſt !

With theſe, the flaming carcaſes conſpire,

To ſcatter ruin, and devouring fire !

** It is very remarkable, the union that ſubſiſted between the ſoldiers and ſailors, during the long, tedious, and dangerous ſiege ; always ready and aƈtive, to ſupport and aſſiſt each other, and ſeem'd never better pleaſed, than when an opportunity offer'd of exerting themſelves for each other : as if fir'd by emulation, who cou'd ſhow themſelves moſt alert, to gain a glorious name, and ſtand with the moſt intrepid ſouls, the greateſt ſhock of danger.

Britiſh,

Britifh, and Gallic guns, and mortars found;
With roar deftructive, fhake th' adjacent ground!
Shrieks! groans! and yells! and hoftile fhouts!
   are heard around!
Such noife heard Satan, (that deceiver fell;)
When on the verge of chaos, night, and hell.
With eager fpeed, they guns, and mortars ply:
And thronging deaths, of lead, and iron fly!
Our troops roar death, againft the batter'd walls!
And death, receive again, from fretful Gauls!

As moles, to fubterraneous holes betake;
So engineers, (unfeen,) approaches make:
Prepar'd (like earthquakes, tumid, from below,
To rife deftructive, with fulphureous glow!
And raze the town, and fort, with inftant overthrow!
Wolfe, and his troops, (with flow advances) fteal,
Towards the town, ftill anxious to prevail.
Saunders, inceffant plies his double tiers:
Makes breach, on breach, and multiplies their fears!

With full ten thoufand, Montcalm keeps the trench:
Canadians, mix'd with trembling, tim'rous French!
Quebec holds out, and much furrender dreads;
Wolfe fhakes his flaming veng'ance o'er their heads!
Confcious of Britifh blood, by murder fpilt!
Of treaties broke! and fportive fcalping guilt!
Of mothers ripp'd, and helplefs infants cries! ⎫
Which calls for fweeping judgment from the fkies! ⎬
They roll with gloomy dread, their haggard eyes! ⎭

Mean while, brave Amherft, Johnfton, Rogers,
        warm
With native zeal, the Continent alarm!
Townfhend, and Bradftreet, Prideaux, Howe, ad-
        vance;
With Forbes, Schomberg, 'gainft the friends of
        France.
Braddick, and Abercromby, bold, arofe;
And wag'd unequal war, againft our foes.

                                        Amherft

Amherſt drove on, cloath'd in ſtern war's alarms!

And ſpread the terror of Britannia's arms!

(Thro' pathleſs dangers; and thro' deep defiles,)⎤

From ambuſh fafe, and bafe Canadian wiles; ⎬

He paſt victorious, heav'n propitious ſmiles! ⎦

So Hannibal, o'er Alpine mountains ſped,

And Carthaginians againſt the Romans led!

Before him forts, towns, corn, and plenty ſtood!⎤

Behind, black defolation might be view'd! ⎬

Bulwarks unmann'd! and trenches drench'd in ⎦

    blood!

Canadian carnage, round the rampiers lay!

And treach'rous Gallic blood, mark'd out his way!

Provincials rage, and Britiſh heroes glow,

For grand revenge, againſt the ſcalping foe!

And like that death, which much fam'd Milton made,

Whom Satan found amid th' infernal ſhade;

And told him ſtraight, he ſhou'd mankind devour,

He bleſs'd his maw, and wiſh'd the happy hour;

Grinn'd horrid fmiles! and brandifh'd high his dart!

Prepar'd to ftrike each living creature's heart!

So thefe rejoice, (inrag'd,) with vengeful gloom!

Anticipate the day, and fix Canadia's doom!

They burn within, with fierce, and martial treads,

Their broad fwords draw, and wave 'em o'er their

heads!

They knit their brows, and with a ftern difdain,

They frown defiance thro' the hoftile plain !

For favage Montcalm, in their minds remain'd,

Who tamely ftood, while Gallic Indians ftain'd

With Britifh conquer'd blood, Fort William's *

plains,

Ripp'd mothers up, and dafh'd out infants brains !

As

---

* When Fort William, (as well as I can remember,) was taken in America, by Monfieur Montcalm, after the furrender of the fort, and our troops were marching out, (according to capitulation :) the Indians fell upon our foldiers, as they paffed on, with their wives and children, and began to knock down, ftrip, and butcher, men, women, and children, promifcuoufly! whilft Monfieur Montcalm, and the French troops, ftood and looked tamely on the difperfion! confufion! and carnage of the Englifh! and on being afked by fome gentlemen, (who fled to them, and claim'd their protection,) why they fuffered this outrage, and cruelty? Montcalm, anfwered them in a frivolous manner, fomething to this purport: that they were a defperate, favage fort of people; fcarcely to be kept within bounds; their good friends and allies, ferved them for what plunder they could get; and claimed it as their due; (tho' fore againft his will;)

and

As when fierce tygers roar amid the wood,

Hunting for prey, full fcent on human blood;

The trav'ller hears, and wing'd with dread furprize!

To diftant fhelter, for his fafety flies!

So veng'ance Amherft roar'd, the French and In-

dians creep,

To woods, and caves, and forts, like flocks of

tim'rous fheep!

Now on the wings of time, the morn appear'd,

Whofe dread approach, Quebec fo greatly fear'd.

When Montcalm, and his troops, fhou'd quit the

field :

To Monckton, Wolfe, and Townfhend, vanquifh'd

·yield !

and as the cafe ftood, they being fo refolute, and ungovern-
able, he could not well tell how to reſtrain them. However,
fevcral who efcaped in the general tumult, fled back to him,
and had the great humanity fhown them, to be preferved
from butchery. Whilft the Indians, ftill continued to glut
themfclves, in plundering, fcalping, ripping womens bodies,
and dafhing childrens brains out! at leaſt, if all this was not
done there; it was done at other places feveral times.

The

The martial trine, afcend the hoftile hill,

The troops infpir'd, a manly ardour feel !

They clamber up, the afcent, rough, and fteep;

Retarded oft, and oft times forc'd to creep!

From bough, to bough, themfelves they onward
        drew;

Their refolution, with the danger grew !

Moft nobly rouz'd, to act beyond compare !

And fhow the world, how much true Britons dare !

To give the French, another fpecimen,

Like Poictiers, Creffy, Blenheim, Dettingen!

And like the (fturdy,) Britifh troops of old;

With whom the Henrys oft the Gauls controul'd;

Onward they trod, with great heroic glow,

To hew thro' fquadrons of the num'rous foe !

Who from a four gun fort, to flight betake,

As Wolfe, and Monckton, their approaches make;

With which our troops, the flying Frenchmen rake!

Rapid as torrents, when they downward fweep!

Howe, and his corps, afcend the rocky fteep,

                They

They clear'd the path, the guards diflodg'd purfu'd,

And all our troops upon the fummit ftood.

There undifturb'd they rang'd, in dread array !

E'er Phœbus thither roll'd the car of day.

Their near approach, alarm'd the threaten'd town,

And now, death wore, a formidable frown !

He fill'd the battlements of hoftile walls ;

To right, and left fuftain'd, by troops of Gauls !

Canadians black, fill'd up the howling rear :

And female fhrieks, and tremor, and pale fear;

And fhatter'd flaming domes, clofe at their heels

     appear !

Now Montcalm, dares t' evacuate the trench :

(Six thoufand Britons brave, ten thoufand French.)

Montcalm, whofe name is brought, by fame, from

     far ;

In battle brave ! and much expert in war !

On

On whom, all France, and Lewis, had an eye;

On whofe try'd conduct, chiefly they rely!

Montcalm! who had fo long, great Wolfe with-
    ftood;

And as a dam, repels a mighty flood;

(Well vers'd in war, back'd by Canadian force,

Stopp'd the brave warrior, in his rapid courfe!

Thus at a bay, retarded, not repell'd;

Cape Breton's fcourge, and England's troops were
    held!

Nought can the will of mighty fate oppofe;

For Montcalm dares, and Wolfe with ardour glows!

The hour is come, and now their eager feet!

Advance with fpeed, in fierce affault to meet;

And with a hoftile frown, each other greet!

So Anthony, dar'd Cefar once t' oppofe;

And ne'er fince then, till now, met two fuch foes!

At ftake, on fortune of the doubtful day,

Canadia's weal, and Britain's honour lay.

                              Tho'

Tho' the spruce Gauls, and Indians, rudely sneer'd,

And ask'd how Wolfe, and his eight thousand dar'd,

To come so far, against their strong Quebec;

Drawn by fond hope, to give their arms a check?

Advis'd he'd go, and this for truth report;

I can't attack, much less reduce the fort;

For Montcalm occupies the hostile plain;

Whose camp I cannot force*, nor charge* sustain!

Wolfe, like a lion growl'd, when held at bay;

And roar'd an answer, on this fatal day.

** On the arrival of Admiral Saunders, with General Wolfe, and the troops near Quebec, when the French understood he had bnt 8000 troops with him, it is reported, they almost sneer'd at him with disdain; confiding in the lofty, and strong situation of the place; and the almost double number of regulars, they had entrench'd near the town, at the only attackable spot, under a bold, enterprising, and fortunate General; Monsieur de Montcalm, and asked where he had left the keys of Quebec? and in a taunting manner, wou'd have him return, and ask his king for them; for he cou'd not force the bars of their gates: not daring to approach near enough; because Monsieur de Montcalm occupied the vacant plain, and formed a living outwork round their rampart, too dreadful for his near approaches; and before whose war he cou'd not stand, if he chose to evacuate the trenches, and give him battle! but how contrary, the great, (and almost unhoped for) event, of all these vaunts was, every one is so well acquainted with it, that it needs no recital here. And I wish I could say, needs no grief, for the loss of so great a patriot, and brave commander.

With

With refted arms, behold our troops advance,

To meet the coming num'rous troops of France.

The Highlanders difcharg'd, their broad fword
      drew ;

And clofe to battle, with the Frenchmen flew !

The reft, as fiercely charg'd the troops of Gaul:

When lo, Wolfe's wrift, was broken by a ball.

(Sound was his heart,) he wrapp'd it up undreft !

And (unconcern'd) among the foremoft preft !

Like to a lion, whom the dogs furround,

By hunters vex'd, and rouz'd by painful wound;

The fearlefs beaft, does all their terrors dare,

He growls, and foams, and fhakes his fhaggy hair !

Aloft they ftand, nor dare provoke the fight ;

He roars aloud, with new collected might !

With rage indignant now, his tail he fwings !

He looks ! and in a ftorm of death he fprings !

O'er dogs, and horfe, and men, his courfe is bent'

Whofe bodies ftrew the way, the gen'rous favage
      went !

                      Thus

Thus with a rage, moft lion like, he turn'd!

His indignation, 'gainft the Frenchmen burn'd!

So Wolfe, and Britons, pierc'd the French array!⎤

And breathlefs carcafes point out his way! ⎬

Where-e'er he turns, death finds an ample prey!⎦

Thoufands recede, and thofe who dare to ftand,

Are hewn in lanes, by his victorious band!

A wound, e'er long, a fecond bullet gave,

And in his belly, dug a fanguin'd grave.

(Fearing his wounds might fpread a wild difmay!

And fix the dubious fortune of the day :)

With well diffembled eafe, he onward trod,

Whilft crimfon'd life, (unfeen,) in torrents flow'd!

In that dread fight! at fam'd Thermopylæ!

So * ebb'd the Spartan's ftream of life away!

Whilft

* Long after Leonidas, (the gallant king of Lacedæmon, in the battle at the pafs of Thermopylæ,) had received a wound in his flank; he ftill rufh'd on, bore nations down! thinn'd the thick wedg'd growing ranks of Barbarians! and roll'd the
Afian

I

Whilft he alone, (with hoftile hofts inclos'd,)

Hew'd wafteful voids ! and all their pow'r oppos'd !

Who, (tho' a king, in freedom's glorious caufe,)

Fell a glad victim, for his country's laws !

Millions of thronging darts, obfcur'd the fkies ! ⎫

He falls, all o'er one wound, no more to rife ! ⎬

Fixt as a rock, his fame ! his honour never dies ! ⎭

So bleeding Wolfe march'd, on without difmay !

To glory's goal, he mark'd his purple way !

But ah! alas! 'gainft fate, what proof is found !

His manly breaft, receives a mortal wound !

Tho' finking down, amid the gloom of death,

The patriot's bofom glow'd with martial wrath !

And whilft the fhades of night upon him fteal,

Moft anxioufly demands, Do we prevail ?

He heard we did, and e'er the hero dy'd,

He own'd himfelf compleatly fatisfy'd !

Afian legions back confounded, with his impetuous charge !
till faint with lofs of blood, and pain, his body throng'd with
wounds, o'erwearied with the long continued battle, almoft
fated with flaughter, and born down by millions, he fell, a noble inftance of that magnanimity, with which the fpirit of freedom animates a patriot's foul !

Cato,

Cato, felf wounded dy'd, and fcorn'd to yield:

But Wolfe, was flain, amid the glorious field!

Th' unwelcome fatal news, to England flies;

And whilft the loud acclaims of joy arife,

For conqueft, on Canadia's cruel fhore;

They mourn the hero, and his lofs deplore!

Maternal fondnefs, heart felt grief exprefs'd!

And all the mother, ftood to view confefs'd!

Fondly abforpt! fhe feem'd, in briny woe!

And fympathizing Britain felt the blow!

The mighty, warlike GEORGE, too condefcends,

To own his worth, and royal pity blends!

Then figh'd, the much renowned Ligonier!

Heroes hold heroes, eminently dear!

The much lov'd Pitt, his eloquence difplay'd,

In due encomiums, on the worthy dead!

Such was his rhet'rick! fuch the force of truth!

So great the actions of the gen'ral's youth!

In lords, and commons, fuch the grateful flame!

They vote a monument of lafting fame!

With glorious truth, his honour to difplay!

Till marble blocks, (themfelves,) fhall fade away!

The living leaders, gain'd a due regard!

Brunſwick applauds! and Britain ſhouts reward!

Each patriot mourn'd! each warring leader ſigh'd!

E'en cowards griev'd, when Wolfe, the hero dy'd.

Among the fair ones, plaintive murmurs ran;

We've loſt the ſoldier! warrior! gentleman!

A ſullen gloom, invades the Engliſh coaſt,

One of our brighteſt conſtellations loſt!

Yet from our ſouls, he never ſhall depart;

Moſt glorioully intomb'd in ev'ry heart!

The Plebeian * crowd, a grateful ardour felt;

And nobly, with his mournful parent dealt.

Adjacent great ones *, ſcorn'd to be outdone, ⎤

Politely penſive, mourn'd her worthy ſon : ⎥
⎬
No fires * there blaz'd! nor bright illuminations ⎥

    ſhone ! ⎦

. But all in ſecret, (with accuſtom'd light,)

Pity, applaud, and oft recount the fight !

*** I often heard it reported, that the common people, (when news came that Quebec was taken, and General Wolfe killed;) generouſly refus'd to ring, make any bonfires, or any kind of tumultous joy, where General Wolfe's mother lived; and that the people of ſuperior rank around her, as politely and generouſly refuſed to make an illumination; but ſullenly ſeem'd to ſympathize, and ſhare her grief. A noble generoſity !

To

To neighb'ring nations, this your fame fhall found,

In fad regret, the gen'ral joy was drown'd.

This fhow'd your value for the patriot more,

Than blazing joy, join'd with deep throated roar.

By ftriplings (now,) in future days grown old,

This pleafing tale, fhall to their fons be told;

Whilft Wolfe's fad mother, for her darling wept,.

The tumult round her dome, in mute oblivion flept!

Hail happy woman! mother of a fon!

Who may be equall'd! never be outdone!

This be thy boaft, thy fon, (Britannia's pride!)

Like great Leonidas *, and Titus † dy'd!

G 2   Their

---

* Leonidas was a Spartan king, defcended from Hercules;
who offered to facrifice his life, that Lacedæmon might not be
entirely deftroyed by Xerxes, who made an attack upon their
countries and liberties, with an army of about four or five millions : and as the Delphic oracle had foretold, a king defcended
from Hercules muft die, to preferve their conntry; Leonidas
immediately repaired to that important pafs, of the much famed
Thermopylæ, with three hundred of his countrymen; who,
with the forces of fome other cities of the Peloponnefus, together with the Thebans, Thefpians, and the troops of thofe
ftates;

Their dying arms, gave num'rous foes a check!

Thy dying fon, was conq'ror at Quebec!

At noon of life, his glory's race was run!

Bright as meridian blaze, his fetting fun!

England will ever hold his mem'ry dear!

From age, to age, the name of Wolfe revere!

For Wolfe firft rofe, and with a dreaded frown,

Rufh'd on the Gauls, and prefs'd toward the town!

ftates; compofed an army, of near eight thoufand men. With
thefe he oft engaged, flew, trod down, and chafed the Afians!
who might be called a hoft of armies! but for the laft fatal encounter, he referved only about fourteen hundred with him,
viz. about three hundred Spartans; four hundred Thebans;
and feven hundred Thefpians. With thefe he moft bravely
attacked the camp of Xerxes, forced his way to the royal pa-
vilion! burnt half the camp! and made an incredible flaughter!
but at length he fell, overpowered by millions! not till he
might almoft be called a conqueror, even in the center of the
enemy's camp.

    † Titus was a young Roman warrior, fon to Æmilius, con-
ful of Rome, and governor of Aquileia; and endued with that
magnanimity, and fpirit of freedom, and valour, for which the
antient Romans were fo much famed. He made a vigorous fally
on the camp of Maximin; fuftained by his brother Paulus, and
the valiant Gartha, a Numidian officer in the troops of Æmi-
lius. Gartha returned wounded from the battle: Paulus and
Titus, the two brothers, were furrounded by an hoft of foes;
born down, and taken prifoners; not till they had formed an
heap of carnage round them, and burnt the tower raifed againft
the wall of Aquileia. But by means of the impetuous rage of
the Britifh legions, in the camp of Maximin, headed by Va-
rus, whom Maximin flew; they were fet at liberty, and Titus
at the head of their refiftlefs war, flew Maximin. But e'er the
battle clofed, received his mortal wound, and died in Aquileia.

                                     And

And with his little army, dar'd advance,

Againſt ten thouſand regulars of France.

(With many Indian tribes, drawn from afar,

For ſcalping, ambuſh, and the butch'ring war.

But theſe, to combat fair, ſcarce ever dar'd,

Where biting Caledonian broad ſwords glar'd.

To ambuſcades they run, in ſhade they lie ;

Nor ſtand the light'ning of an Engliſh eye !)

As billows ſpread, when daſhing on a rock ;

(Which ſtands unmov'd, amid the pond'rous ſhock;)

They fall in froth, and foam on ev'ry ſide,

Blended, and loſt, amidſt the briny tide.

So when their troops, our frowning troops beheld;

Receiv'd their ſhock, and found themſelves repell'd;

And ſaw fierce Highlanders, their broad ſwords

  · wield !

They ſoon fell off, diſorder'd, thro' the field !

Now fell brave Wolfe ! whoſe preſence oft. inſpir'd

With emulating glow ! and ev'ry warrior fir'd !

The

The brave defenders of Britannia's weal;

Which fought round Wolfe, and saw grim death
　　prevail,

Rous'd by efteem, and love! with mighty rage!

Prepar'd moft fiercely, with the foe t' engage!

Each lov'd the man! the warrior all efteem'd!

Their leader! friend! and martial! father deem'd!

Revenge! revenge! injur'd Britannia calls!

As mighty cat'racts roar from lofty falls!

They fhout! unite! and rufh upon the Gauls!

And like a pond'rous overwhelming flood!

They fwept along! and glutted death with food!

And Frenchmen mourn'd Wolfe's fall, in ftreams
　　of blood!

Howe, and his infantry*, amidft the doubtful
　　field,

Round the left flank, and rear, in femicircle wheel'd;

A living rampart form'd, a fierce offenfive fhield!

* It is faid, in an account of the battle, that Col. Howe
with his light infantry, covered the left wing and rear in fuch a
manner, as entirely to fruftrate the attempts of the enemy's Indians, and Canadians, upon that flank.

By

By thefe, the charging enemy, were oft repell'd;
Broken, difpers'd, o'eraw'd, and at due diftance
   held!
Or down in carnage trod, in clofe engagement fell'd!

E'er Gallia's troops, to wild diforder yield;
Reluétant next, brave Monckton quits the field.
Oft frowning turn'd, and ey'd the hoftile Gauls;
Like great Eneas, near Laurentum's walls.
Soldiers, and failors, jointly, all agreed,
Bold Monckton wou'd have done, what Townfhend
   did.
Did Townfhend's bofom, glow with martial flame,
Monckton had ardour, equal to the fame.
Did Townfhend brave th' impetuous Gallic wrath!
So Monckton dar'd! midft fhow'rs of leaden death!
Was Townfhend there, a Gen'ral in command;
In that exalted rank, might Monckton ftand.
Was honour, death, or viét'ry, Townfhend's áim!
Conqueft, or death, was gallant Monckton's claim!

Each

Each with indiff'rence, hoftile dangers view'd;

And the great end, with fouls refolv'd purfu'd.

Monckton led on, to fierce encounter bent;

Till thro' his lungs, the rapid ball was fent.

Th' ill fated bullet, nipt his foul's defign,

And fent him wounded, from th' advancing line.

He fain wou'd reap the honour of the day;

But fate demands him from the glorious fray!

As fierce Achilles, on the Phrygian plain,

When brave Patroclus, was by Hector flain;

And fage Ulyffes, from the battle fent,

Came limping, wounded, near the hero's tent;

Frowning rufh'd on, in mighty tranfport toft!

And with his pow'rs, rejoin'd the friendly hoft!

He, and his myrmidons, like torrents flow'd!

Repell'd! bore down! and o'er the Trojans trod!

So Townfhend, and his troops, to battle throng!

And urge the war, triumphantly along!

Here Townſhend's ſkill, and heroiſm ſhone!
Two Gen'rals dropp'd, and he was left alone,
To lead, encourage, cheer each ſoldier's mind!
A work, ev'n three, an arduous taſk wou'd find!

Howe! Murray! Fraſer! Burton! Dalling, bold!
Like ſparkling gems, in bars of poliſh'd gold,
'Mongſt hardy ranks, conſpicuouſly appear!
In front, in flanks, the center, or the rear!
Macdonald! Ince! with equal glory ſhine!
Fam'd in the glorious war of fifty nine!
Leaders, and ſoldiers, with one warring ſoul,
Thro' blood, and flame, and death to honour's gaol,
Onward they plung'd, with veng'ance fiercely pleas'd!
With ſanguin'd graſp'd, the palm of vict'ry ſeiz'd!
The dying Wolfe, the ſhouts of conqueſt heard!
The welcome ſound, the bleeding Monckton chear'd!

As when a gen'rous bull, has broke his chain,
Lays heaps, on heaps, o'er all the frighted plain,

Sweeps

Sweeps thro' the throng, and with refiftlefs wrath,

Spurns, toffes, gores, and tramples crowds to death!

So, thro' the ranks of war, Macpherfon hew'd!

With martial foul, and manly arm endu'd!

Tho' with the weight of weak'ning years oppreft,

Finds youthful ardour glowing in his breaft!-

That weight of years, no longer feems to feel;

But deals out death, with bright avenging fteel!

Or as the Sons of Scotland, once before,

When they defcended on Cape Breton's fhore;

Forc'd thro' the French, with fierce Herculean
    might,

And triumph'd 'midft the dangers of the fight!

He lifts his fword, and with repeated blow,

As peafants thro' a field of barley mow,

He lays the Gauls in heaps, in fanguin'd over-
    throw!

This faw our troops, and quick, from man, to man,

(As trains of powder blaze,) an ardour ran!

Grown greatly emulous, (with fixed thought,)

Each like a Hector, or Achilles fought!

The

The Anstruthers and Scots, with mutual wrath!
In Frenchmens bodies oft, their broad swords
    sheath !
And onward tread, amid refulgent death !
Where'er they turn'd, a transient brightness gleam'd;
Which like th' aurora borealis seem'd !

Mean while, each diff'rent corps for fight addrest;
With fixed bayonets, to stand the test.
As bolts, and lightnings, rive the knotted oak,
Thro' thick throng'd ranks, of charging French-
    men broke !
As they grew warm, the Frenchmens hearts grew
    cold,
Platoons of soldiers, o'er the leaders roll'd !
Before the English charge, (with Gallic dread,)
Cohorts receding tumbled o'er the dead !

Battalions,

Battalions, and brigades, were * throng'd with fouls
    transfix'd !

In heaps, the fighting, wounded, dying, dead,
    were mix'd !

And as in whirlwinds, on Arabia's coaft,

(Amid furprize!) whole caravans are loft !

So thefe born down, before the Britifh might,

(Involv'd in fear,) their fafety fought in flight.

Now Montcalm flees, amidft a total rout !

(Canadians yell! and conq'ring Britons fhout!

And fpread tumultous terror round about !

He thought, (like floods, when fwoln by heavy
    fhow'rs,)

Begirt with Gauls, and black Canadian pow'rs,

To fweep triumphant, o'er the Indian plains ;

Gave favage rage, and cruelty the reins.

The mighty pond'rous tafk, he could not wield ;

Nor cou'd Quebec from Albion's thunder fhield !

* It is faid, in one defcription of the battle, that the French
troops, oft throng'd in heaps, at the repeated charges of our
infantry; till at length they fcatter'd, and commenc'd a total
rout, in the ufual French manner, full fpeel to the town.

                        Wolfe,

Wolfe, and his feconds, flung him vanquifh'd down!

And chas'd his troops, diforder'd to the town!

Now death, with implements, was amply ftor'd;

Lurk'd in a halbert, pike, fpontoon, or fword.

In guns, and piftols too, he oft was found! ⎫

And flafh'd out fate, with moft unwelcome found! ⎬

And oft, a broad fword, gave the deadly wound! ⎭

Bougainville's * corps, now threaten'd in the rear,

Frefh troops, with formidable front appear.

As if they wou'd, the nice occafion catch,

And from our troops, the infant vict'ry fnatch.

To take their charge, and their defign to mar,

Ours fac'd about, and met the coming war:

* M. de Bougainville, whom the feign'd movements of the Englifh troops, had drawn up the river, turn'd back on difcovering their real defign; and now appear'd on the rear of the army, with a body of 2000 men. But fortunately, the main body of the French, was by this time fo broken and difperfed, that the General was able to eftablifh his rear, and to turn fuch an oppofiti n on that fide, that the enemy retir'd after a very feeble attempt.

With

With efforts weak, they faintly ſtood the teſt;
Soon wheel'd, retir'd, and ran to join the reſt.

The angry warriors, throng towards the town!
Midſt flame! and blood! and groans! tread French-
    men down!
Quite to the ditch, beneath Quebec's ſtrong walls!
They chas'd! ran down! and kill'd the trembling
    Gauls!
The town ſubmitted, ſtruck with dread ſurprize!
Aloft the croſs, the Britiſh enſign flies!
There may it fly! there Britiſh cannon roar!
Till wolves leave prey! and Gauls deceive no more!
Amen.

ON

ON that great day, Wolfe's warring fpirit

fled!

And Monckon, for his King, and Country

bled!

When conq'ring Townfhend, chac'd the flying Gauls!

And terror fhook, Quebec's exalted walls!

Whilft leading fiercely on, to toilfome fight,

Cohorts of heroes, 'gainft unequal might.

A brave old man, judicious Townfhend ey'd :

Mark'd how his fword, with Gallic crimfon dy'd,

Rofe like a comet *, with his flaming train!

And glar'd deftruction thro' the hoftile plain!

How oft alternate * rofe! how oft it fet!

And fetting, fell'd a Frenchman * at his feet!

Saw him behind the heaps of flain retire,

To breathe awhile *, and with collected ire,

Saw him again, addrefs himfelf to fight ;

Hew *! and tread down! and put the foe to flight!

He

***** In the battle, before the town of Quebec; we had an
account, of Malcolm Macpherfon, a brave old Highlander,
whom

He fmil'd, o'erjoy'd! to fee th' old man advance
Amid the carnage, of deceitful France!
With pleafing horror! view'd the heaps of dead,
Around the worthy Caleaonian fpread!

whom General Townfend obferv'd, (after the Generals, Wolfe,
and Monckton, were carried out of the line,) laying about him
with uncommon fury; and likewife, (tho' he fo often lifted
his fword, he fcarce dealt a blow in vain: but at every ftroke,
he fell'd a Frenchman at his feet! the account further fays,
that General Townfhend mark'd when he retir'd behind the
heaps of flain, (lain dead by his own hand,) to breathe awhile,
as if glutted with deftruction! and fatiated with flaughter! and
faw him pull off his coat, or jacket, and with an heroic ardour,
glowing anew, (like an active flame, which had juft overcome
all oppofition,) hew his way thro' thick throng'd obftructing
ranks of Frenchmen! bearing down, or putting to flight, who-
e'er came within the femi-zone, form'd by his tremendous
fword! after the battle, General Townfhend afk'd his name,
age, and place of abode, or country. He anfwer'd, his name
was Macpherfon: came from the Highlands of Scotland; and
his age was feventy-two. The fword he then fought with, had
been in the family about three hundred years: he efteem'd it
almoft as his life; and feem'd exceedingly alert! and well
pleas'd! that he had us'd it on that memorable day fo well,
againft the enemies of Caledonia! General Townfhend, infpir'd with noble fentiments of the brave old hero's worth, reported his gallant behaviour to his Majefty; and feconded it
with the honeft rhetorick of a great foul'd commander, and a
gentleman foldier! and it is well known, in all the Britifh do-
minions, fuch his Majefty loves; who not forgetting the martial fire of his own youth! (of which Dettingen remains a glorious inftance!) gave him his royal favour, and a commiffion;
b which he is for the future, intitled to the character of Malcolm Macpherfon, Gent. And it is faid, the people of London
were not behind hand, in their gratitude; but when he pafs'd,
wou'd cry out with a pleafing exclamation! there goes the gallant Scotchman! the intrepid Highlander! who laid the French
in heaps, at the battle of Quebec! God blefs the brave old boy,
with his broad fword! &c.

Conceiv'd

Conceiv'd him ftraight the terror of the day!
Defign'd by fate, to glut grim death with prey!

The battle o'er, our troops return'd from chace;
Townfhend demands his age, his name, and place.
Stern he reply'd! Macpherfon is my name!
From Scotia's hills, a volunteer I came.
Years, feventy-two, their influence have fhed,
And roll'd fucceffive, o'er my hoary head.
This fword I wield, now ftain'd with hoftile gore,
For near three hundred years, my fathers wore;
Good northern temper'd fteel! a trufty blade!
With which my anceftors great havoc made!
This I hold dear! this as my life I prize!
(And terrors glanc'd from both the warrior's eyes!)

This Royal GEORGE, from Townfhend, quickly
    knew;
Who gave the brave old hero all his due!

Out

Our martial King, beftows on him regard,

Gives Royal Favour, and a great reward!

Applauding crowds, with joy! his worth proclaim!

And grateful Britain, ecchoes back his fame;

Gallia, no more, we'll threat with hoftile frown,

For GEORGE's fmiles can pull her grandeur down.

Approving Majefty, her fchemes can marr,

And rouze our troops, to glory, and to war!

Whilft with the royal fmile, their labour's crown'd,

In each platoon, fome heroes will be found!

End of B O O K III.

The ARGUMENT.

*Conflans sails from Breft, to invade England. Chafes
Commodore Duff's fquadron. The Chatham, Capt.
Lockhart, aftern of the fleet, near being taken.
His anxiety during the chace : but on feeing Admiral Hawke's fleet, tacks upon the chafing enemy,
(who ftagger'd in their refolutions,) and begins the
chace himfelf. Admiral Hawke bearing down into
the center of the French fleet, finking the Superbe,
and attacking Admiral Conflans; who flees, and
runs on fhore.*

*Capt. Speke, in the Refolution, attacking and taking
the Formidable, the French rear Admiral.*

*Lord Howe, in the Magnanimme, attacking, overpow-
ering, and driving on fhore the Heros.*

*The Hon. Auguftus Keppel, in the Torbay, attacking
and finking the Thefee.*

Capt. Baird, in the Defiance.

Capt. Shirley, in the Kingfton.

Capt. Maplefden, in the Intrepid.

Sir John Bentley, in the Warfpight.

Capt. Storr, in the Revenge.

Capt. Rowley, in the Montague.

Capt. Gambier, in the Burford.

Capt. Dennis, in the Dorfetfhire; and

*Capt. Obrien, in the 'Effex; all bearing down to Ad-
miral Hawke's affiftance, and engaging.*

*The anxiety of the reft of the Captains aftern, who
cou'd not poffibly come into the engagement; crouding
fail, and driving down to battle! the rout! difperfion! and flight of the French fleet, on fhore,
up the river Villaine, &c. Great Britain's joy!
and Gallia in tears! as the confequence of the engagement.*

WAR:

W A R:

B O O K IV.

GALLIA's ill fate, ſtill mightily prevails;
See, next from Breſt, invading Conſlan˄
    ſails;

Of conqueſt dreams, and England over-run;

Like Phæton, mounts the chariot* of the ſun*:

Like him, (triumphant,) wrapp'd in Gallic blaze,

He thought t' have drown'd Britannia in amaze!

But met Hawke's glance, and retrograde retir'd,

And ignis fatuus like, his flame expir'd.

This Lewis, ſuits thy ſchemes on Britain's ſhore,

Thyſelf, thy leaders led, by Pompadour.

  ** Le Soleil Royal, in Engliſh, the Royal Sun. And in
Ovid's Metarphoſes, we have Phæton driving the chariot of the
Sun, and daſh'd from the ſeat by Jupiter.

When firft from Breft, the threat'ning Conflans fail'd,

(In naval war,) he feemingly prevail'd :

He crouded * after Duff †, with eager chace,

Which train'd him on to Hawke, and French dif-

grace !

* It is a common term at fea; when fhips are in full chace, and make what fail they can, that they crouded one after ano- ther, with all the fail they cou'd pack.

† When Admiral Hawke, with the Britifh fleet, firft came in fight of Monfieur Conflans, and the French fleet; he was in full chace of Commodore Duff, and his little fquadron of fri- gates, &c. with the Chatham, Capt. Lockhart among them. The Chatham was aftern of our fleet, and very near the enemy, and confequently, not making that fpeed off, the frigates, and the reft of the fleet did, he muft foon have fall'n into the hands of the enemy ; without fome friendly affiftance from larger fhips, with heavier metal, than what Duff's fquadron carried ; and which in that circumftance, he cou'd fcarce flatter himfelf fhou'd arrive fo foon, (and even unexpectedly,) as it did to England's and his great joy ! brave Hawke's honour ! and thofe bold commanders which were with him ! and to the great lofs and infamy of Conflans, and the Gallic nation ! for had not Admiral Hawke arrived to his affiftance, the moft romantic per- fon living, (with the leaft fhew of reafon,) cou'd not have ex- pected Capt. Lockhart, to have begun a defperate, (and I may fay hopelefs) engagement, with the firft fhip that fhou'd have come up with him ; when there were twenty-one fail of line of battle fhips, bearing down upon him, with three Admirals. But fo foon as Admiral Hawke, and the Englifh fleet appear'd, he tack'd immediately on the headmoft fhips of the chafing enemy ; fingled out the Heros, which had been a little fhattered by fome of our fhips, as they pafs'd, and gave her two broad- fides, e'er fhe ftruck to the Magnanime, Lord Howe, who bore down to clofe engagement with her; and to whom fhe ftruck, but afterwards went on fhore.

Lockhart,

Lockhart, who oft had wond'rous odds oppos'd!

Now deigns to flee, by hoftile odds inclos'd!

In iron wombs, th' unequal war drew near!

Reafon fuggefts his flight, but not his fear.

Had Conflan's felf, the Chatham chas'd alone,

Let Britons judge, what Lockhart wou'd have done!

Perhaps that day, fuch deeds had been atchiev'd,

England might boaft! tho' France, and Britain

      griev'd!

But now he flees, yet with a fullen frown,

He ey'd the fleet, to battle bearing down!

Oft he refolv'd to fight, with wonted glow!

As oft refolv'd, to flee before the foe!

Reafon, and courage, fill'd him with regret!

Like wind, and tide, in raging conflict met!

So flees the lion's cub, toward the den,

From deep mouth'd dogs, and troops of armed men:

Pro-

Promifcuous cries, and fhouts, his ears affail;

Againft his mighty fides, he fwings his tail!

Indignant growls! collected, turns to fight!

Again recedes, and makes a tardy flight.

But now the fire, comes roaring thro' the plain!

He turns, attacks the foremoft of the train!

(Wrath fills his eyes! aloft his tail is rear'd!)

So when to view, Great Britain's fleet appear'd;

Lockhart, with wonted rage, and fierce delight!

Mark'd out the Gallic Hero * for the fight!

Stung with difdain to flee, tho' fleets gave chace;

He long'd to wipe away the late difgrace;

To battle tack'd, upon the chafing Gauls;

And fent in thund'ring fhow'rs, his dafhing balls!

Gave iron proof, urg'd home! convinc'd the enemy,

'Twas mighty odds, mov'd his intrepid foul to

 flee!

* The French fhip Heros, to which he gave two broadfides
before fhe ftruck, to the Magnanime; Lord Howe, and who
engag'd her, and to whom fhe ftruck.

No sooner Hawke, saluted Conflans's sight,

His slacken'd sails, hung shiv'ring * in affright !

Like their commander's, ev'ry ship appear'd ;

And flutt'ring * sails flapp'd out, what Frenchmen
    fear'd !

The chace of Duff, they seemingly repine,

And disconcerted, drew into a line !

  * Whoever has been on the sea, doubtless hath observ'd,
that when a ship luffs up, (as the sailors call it, that is braces
about,) with her head to the wind, with an intent to lye by,
(as they term it.) The topsails, and coursers, shiver in the
wind, and slap against the masts, shrouds, &c. as the ship
plunges, and rolls, for want of a proper head way' thro' the
water. So Conflans, and his fleet, when they hove too ; the
ships might be said to express their terror : on account of the
agitation of their hulls, and the tremor, and shiv'ring of their
sails : (as trembling is generally allow'd to be a true sign of
fear.) And they might be said to be in fear, on another account ; for it was observed, that they drew in o a sort of a
disorder'd line, and seem'd quite confus'd ! like a man on the
brink of an impending precipice, below which, the rugged
rocks rise in dreadful spires, and he condemn'd to plunge precipitate from thence. So Conflans, and his fleet, by their behaviour, seem'd to fluctuate in their intentions ; as if afraid to
fight ! asham'd to run ! and dreading the consequence of an
equal number of line of battle ships, bearing down upon them !
mann'd with Englishmen ! and arm'd with engines, whose
wombs were pregnant with flaming roar ! with iron, and with
leaden death ! ready to burst from ev'ry side, and crush their
navy in oblivion ! and I think the event fully declar'd what
their intentions were, by their behaviour, when the battle began : greatest part of them running away like a terrify'd brood
of chickens, from a Hawk, which souses near them, and scarce
staying even to fight their way ; but made what speed they cou'd
on shore, up the river Villaine, &c.

They

They feem'd to fee their rout, and overthrow,
Whilft waiting for the formidable foe !
Who plung'd promifcuous on, with naval rage!
As if ambitious who fhou'd firft engage.

So when the vulture chafes thro' the air,
A young fledg'd eaglet, (yet the mother's care ;)
The tow'ring bird, (imperial,) from the fkies,
On founding pinions, to his refcue flies :
In dread, the vulture flacks the rapid chace ;
Flutters, and hovers ftill around the place ;
Receives the eagle's fhock, and in affright,
From chafing, fpreads his wings in fhameful flight!

The hoftile fleets, now near each other glide ;
And load with future death, the briny tide !
So high in air, the gath'ring tempeft flies,
In pitchy clouds, (which at a diftance rife ;)

Nearer

Nearer they roll, a gloomy concave form;

Together clafh, down comes the rattling ftorm!

Now wakes the roar, and on the tempeft rolls,

The bolts, and light'nings fly, the thunder growls!

So cannons roar, in clouds the fhips are hid;

And French, and Britifh tars, alternate bleed!

Round, and grape fhot, and barr'd, make dreadful wreck!

Sails, topmafts, men, and blocks, beftrew the deck!

Guns are difmounted! limbs from bodies tore!

Whilft thro' both fides, the rapid bullets bore!

Wide gaps they rend, as thro' the fhips they pafs;

And fhrouds *, and ftays *, hang dangling by the
maft.

The human blood, in crimfon torrents flows!

With fiercer rage, each naval warrior glows!

** The fhrouds, are feveral large ropes, faften'd at the maft-
head, and come down to the larboard, and ftarboard fide; there
faften'd to the chain plates, to fupport the maft, in the rolling
of the fhip, and when they carry fail, and to thefe the rattlings
are fixed, to go to maft-head by. The ftays are much for the
fame ufe, only they come down to the fide, &c. on a flant,
and are defign'd to preferve the maft in its pofition, when the
fhip bounds o'er the waves, or plunges with a fudden jerk from
the fummit of a watry hill, that it may not fall aft, or pitch
forward over the fhip's head.

And

And whilft they eagerly for vict'ry burn,

Volleys, and broadfides (giv'n,) they angrily return

As thund'ring Jove, the wrathful bolts prepar'd;

And wrapp'd in flame, the veng'ance high uprear'd;

With roar impetuous, down the ftorm he hurl'd!

'Gainft Phæton, driving round the burning world.

Unerring roll'd, the great æthereal war!

And dafh'd him from Apollo's flaming car!

So Hawke bore down, amid the Gallic fleet,

And Conflans fought with like affault to greet;

Larboard *, and ftarboard *, ev'ry foe repell'd!

But ftill, the pond'rous war, for Conflans held!

O'er French Magnificence †, victorious drove!

Which in a fruftrate oppofition ftrove:

This Conflans faw, and feem'd on battle bent;

And 'gainft the Royal George a broadfide fent:

** It is the fea term for the right and left fide of the fhip.
† Le Superbe, a French 74 gun fhip, which bore down bravely between the Royal George, and Le Soleil Royal, to oppofe Admiral Hawke, who ftruck her on a careen the firft broadfide, and the fecond broadfide funk her. The name in Englifh is Magnificent, or Magnificence.

Who

Who pour'd his torrents fierce, of flame, and balls!

Struck Conflans mute! (and terrify'd the Gauls!)

Is Phæton drown'd in blaze *, let drop the reins,

And madly drove along th' æthereal plains,

The mighty whirl, opprefs'd his foul with fear!

He fat appall'd *, amid the wild career!

No longer now, the foaming fteeds confines,

Twixt Leo, Urfa, and the Scorpion * figns:

*** The p ets fay, Phæton being told by his mother, he
vas the fon of Phœbus, (that is Apollo,) who drives the radiant
ar of day: he went to the temple of the fun, and being own'd
by his father, who fwore by Styx, to grant his requeft; he de-
manded to drive the chariot of the fun for a day. Phœbus
knowing the great, (and certain) danger of the enterprize,
long time diffuades him from it: but the adventrous youth,
(fir'd by an emulation for glory, and ambitious notions of honour,) vaults into the feat, after much pre-admonition from his
father, who griev'd at the confequence. He drove on, the
horfes foon found their new mafter, (or rather new driver,) by the
unfkillful guidance of the rein, and the chariot wanting its
proper poize. They grew headftrong, and hurried him thro'
the cœleftial regions; now with a rapid flight, defcending
near the earth; again, bounding aloft, they whirl'd him thro'
the immenfe fpace of Æther! then ftarting wide to right and
left, plung'd among the conftellations! he dropped the reins,
and fat appall'd, amidft the career! was afraid to advance, and
cou'd not retreat: but grew terrify'd, amidft the frightful mon-
fters of the fkies! and a new pannic affail d his heart, as the
chariot of the fun approach'd the Scorpion, and when (with
the intenfe heat,) he faw him fweat in his poifon! the confequence of all this is, the Heavens are drain'd of all their moi-
fture; the earth is parch'd; the fea boils to its bed; and all
nature lies gafping in one univerfal calenture! at length, Jove
lifted the avenging bolt; and with unerring aim, fent it wing'd
with lightning, and dafh'd him from Apollo's car!

He

He fear'd t' advance, wou'd backward fain retreat;

And quit Apollo's car, and flaming feat !

So Conflans, from the Bay, wou'd abfent be:

From Hardy, Howe, and frowning Hawke wou'd
    flee !

Backward he drove, whilft pannic fears prevail!

And left the chariot of the bright Soleil * !

Shunn'd the loud ftorm, midft which, brave
    Hawke career'd !

The Britifh bolts, and Englifh light'nings fear'd!

To Gallia's fhore, and certain fhipwreck, fteer'd!

Each fternmoft fhip, to clofer action glides ;

And bellows death, from fulminating fides!

Rouz'd to fee Hawke, midft dangers, fmoak, and
    flame !

They crouded fail, and to the battle came.

* When Admiral Hawke had funk the Superbe, he bore
down upon Conflans, who ftood one broadfide and ran, making a fignal for all the fleet to do the like ; and at laft, rather
than fight Admiral Hawke, he drove on fhore and his fhip
was burnt; after being quitted by Conflans and her crew.

As hungry lions, pawing to engage!

With lafhing tails, will work themfelves to rage!

So thefe, to patriot wrath, their fouls had wrought!

For board, and board, feem'd ev'ry warrior's thought!

The gallant Speke*, with Refolution * arm'd!

True Briton like, for great atchievements warm'd!

Down from the ftaff, the hoftile banner tore;

And filenc'd all the Formidable's * roar!

And Howe†, Magnanimous †! with courage ftor'd!

Bore down, and clapp'd the Heros clofe on board;

Who ftruck, o'erpower'd! no longer dar'd t'engage!

Whilft Thefee ‡ funk beneath brave Keppel's rage!

   *** Capt. Speke commanded his Majefty's fhip Refolution;
engag'd the Formidable; the French rear Admiral, and took
him, after a defperate cannonading.

   †† Lord Howe, in his Majefty's fhip Magnanimme, engaged
the Heros board and board, which in little odds of half an
hour, did fo much execution, that fhe ftruck; but afterwards
drove on fhore.

   ‡ The honourable Auguftus Keppel, in the Torbay, engag'd
the Thefee, and funk her the fecond broadfide.

                                                         Baird,

Baird*, for renown, moft refolutely ftrove !

And thro' the line, with bold Defiance* drove !

Two line of battle fhips, (with hoftile roar,)

Down on his fhip, to clofe engagement bore:

Their joint attack, he bravely ſcorn'd to fhun,

But gave 'em roar, for roar, and gun for gun!

Intrepid † Maplefden †! and Bentley ‡ bold !

Thro' the French line, midft gloomy veng'ance
        roll'd !

Whilft Rowley ‖, Gambier ‖, Dennis ‖, onward
        croud,

Like Jove's artill'ry, in a thunder cloud !

And brave Obrien ‖, join'd the concert loud !

** Capt. Baird, commanded the fhip Defiance, and engag'd.
†† Capt. Maplefden, commanded the fhip Intrepid, and
engag'd.
‡ Sir John Bentley, in the Warfpight, engag'd likewife.
‖‖‖‖‖ Capt. Rowley, in the Montague; Capt. Gambier, in
the Burford; Capt. Dennis, in the Dorfetfhire; and Capt.
Obrien, in the Effex; all likewife engag'd. And here I fhou'd
have mentioned Capt. Campbell: but as I have mention'd Admiral Hawke, in the Royal George; and as 'tis well known
Mr. Campbell is Captain of the Royal George, it may be taken
for granted, Capt. Campbell was in the midft of danger, and
in the very center of the engagement.

                                        Sheirly,

Sheirly *, as bravely join'd the warlike throng!

And hurl'd deſtruction, as he plung'd along!

With England's dread Revenge †, Storr † fiercely
came!

And roar'd out Frenchmen's fate, in Britiſh flame!

Reſolv'd they fought, by Hawke's example fir'd!

And Gallia's fleet, confuſedly retir'd;

Whilſt ſome in tardy blaze, conſume away,

And add new horrors, to the dreadful fray!

Here, lower maſts, are tumbled o'er the ſide,

There ſhips deſcend, amid the briny tide!

Which all their flame, and harmleſs thunder drown'd!

Whilſt Hawke, and Britons ſhout, with conqueſt
crown'd!

Thoſe, whom ill fortune from the fight detain'd,

With viſible regret, aftern remain'd.

(For war they burn'd, with warring hearts elate! ⎫

But mortals cannot guide the hand of fate: ⎬

Altho' their ſouls, the ſhips anticipate! ⎭

* Capt. Sheirly, commanded the Kingſton, and engag'd.
†† Capt. Storr, commanded the Revenge, and engag'd.

When ftern Achilles, (with remorfelefs mind;)

The field * of fame! the toils of war * declin'd!

Between the rampart, and the fwelling flood,

The fretful Myrmidonian leaders ftood.

Oft as they heard the animating fhout!

Oft as they faw the Grecians put to rout!

As oft their mighty fouls, were in a glow!

To rufh all clad with death, upon the chafing foe!

So thefe croud on, vex'd with heroic rage!

To fee their friends, and countrymen engage.

At each broadfide, they glow'd with fiercer flame!

To reap the harveft of immortal fame!

** In the fixteenth book of Homer's Iliad, we have Achilles, fpeeding from tent to tent, and warming the hearts of the myrmidonian leaders, juft going to battle, (to fave the Grecian fleet,) under the conduct of Patroclus; and we have them and the troops reprefented as ftanding round their chief. A grim! terrific! formidable band! like voracious wolves, rufhing a hideous throng, to flake their thirft, after a glut of flaughter! and prefent a deathful view! and we may judge of their uneafinefs and regret, at being detain'd from the battle, by the expreffions which Achilles ufes to them; calling them for fam'd! fierce! and brave myrmidons! tells them to think with what threats they dar'd the Trojans! and what reproach his ears had fo long endur'd! calling him ftern fon of Peleus! whofe rage defrauded them of fo fam'd a field! &c. and adds, lo! there the Trojans! this day fhall give you all your fouls demand! &c.

For

For defp'rate battle, ev'ry bofom burn'd!

The tardy progrefs of the veffels mourn'd.

The topmafts bend! fails fplit! and halliards break!

The dormant thunder, on each well clear'd deck,

In hollow tubes, from ev'ry yawning fide,

Portended dreadful! o'er the fwelling tide!

Each Britifh tar well pleas'd, to quarters ftood! ⎫

(And ponder'd on the future fcene of blood! ⎬

As on they labour'd thro' the briny flood! ⎭

No difcontented tar like hints we hear,

As if they lagg'd, infpir'd by grov'ling fear.

No lack of courage, to their charge is laid;

They caught each blaft; each ufeful fail was fpread.

Full on the Gallic line, refolv'd they fteer'd;

Who tack'd, made fail, the clofe engagement fear'd!

Each brave commander, martial zeal expreft,

And long'd to bring his honour to the teft!

Seem'd anxious, fome refolved foe to meet,

But night came on, and fav'd the Gallic fleet,

Againft

Againſt the yielding foe, our tars complain'd ;

And ſlighted conqueſt, eaſily obtain'd.

Each man was full of cool delib'rate rage !

And hop'd the French wou'd ſturdily engage.

Shot, ſtores, and guns, they ſunk amid the main !

And fled for ſafety, to the ſhoal Villaine !

Britain rejoic'd ! perfidious Gallia mourn'd !

Her royal navy, taken, ſunk, or burn'd !

Her cities, forts, iſles, towns, and all her ſchemes

    o'erturn'd !

End of **B O O K IV.**

The

The ARGUMNNT.

Britannia represented clad in terrors! and leaning on
Pitt; (like Achilles, reclin'd on his spear, after the
carnage he had made among the Trojans, in revenge
for the death of Patroclus.) A recapitulation of
Great Britain's victories, both by sea and land, and
the French terror! Thurot rushing forth to war
against the English, (like a tyger, to hunt his prey,
without his teeth and claws.) His landing on the
Irish coast. Taking Carrickfergus, and laying Bel-
fast under contribution. The Hibernian zeal and
bravery of the few troops there; rending the bat-
tlements of the castle of Carrickfergus, and fling-
ing the stones on the enemy for some time, after all
their ammunition was spent! the consternation of
the French at their intrepidity! their sullen submis-
sion; (like our gallant troops at Cas.) The
French retreat, and reimbarkation. Their joy
damp'd, (like the Amalekites, who spoil'd Ziklag,)
when the Captains, Elliott, Clements, and Logie,
in the Æolus, Brilliant, and Pallas, bore down to
engage. The fight, and Thurot's death; with the
French submission. An address to Lewis, with a
recital of the gallantry of our matchless tars, and
intrepid troops! a few similies on George the Se-
cond; like eagle mounted Jove, directing the thun-
der against Gaul, &c. &c. &c.

WAR:

W   A   R:

B O O K   V.

BRitannia, (long, for feats of arms renown'd,)
In terrors clad! with num'rous vict'ries
crown'd!

Leaning on Pitt, as if to breathe awhile ;

She ftood, and caft a fierce indignant fmile!

Like great Achilles, on his fpear reclin'd,

The war revolving, in his martial mind!

Moft greatly pleas'd! 'twixt rage, and ftern difdain !

He·fmiling, frown'd, acrofs the Phrygian plain !

O'er flaughter'd heaps of Trojans by him flain !

So ftood Britannia, pleas'd, ferene, fedate !

Compleatly arm'd! victoriously elate!

Her dreadful fhores, appear'd one hallow'd bound! ⎫
Her horfe, and foot, rang'd on her frontier ground! ⎬
Her navy girded her with terrors round! ⎭

At diftance ftood, (as thunderftruck!) the Gaul;
Amidft Quebec's, and Louifbourg's downfall!
Goree, and Guadaloupe, in ruin lay!
And Senegal, had felt the like difmay!

Their fleets cou'd not our fleets attack fuftain! ⎫
Some at Lagos, fome founder'd at Villaine! ⎬
Some burnt, fome funk, amid the fwelling main! ⎭

A pannic dread, prevail'd at land, and fea! ⎫
They ftruck, or fled, in fwift affright away! ⎬
As doves from Jove's imperial bird of prey! ⎭

They turn'd their backs, (as wonted,) to the chace:
All fear'd, at leaft few dar'd, to fhow their face!
Till Thurot rofe, (to hide the Gallic fhame;)
And rafhly fir'd, fail'd forth to gain a name:
And like a tyger, from his lurking den,
Rufh'd on, fupported by a thoufand men:
But in fuch plight, to back his daring caufe,
He feem'd to hunt his prey, without his teeth, and
        claws!

Of

Of this, (perhaps,) the Gaul will proudly boaft;

He landed on Hibernia's naked coaft!

So cowards, may the lion's den affail,

And boaft from thence, the new whelp'd cubs they
     fteal;

Whilft both old lions, thro' the foreft roam,

And fearch for prey, far diftant from their home:

But fhou'd loud roar, befpeak the lions near,

As if their final knell, had pierc'd their ear,

They fteal, (nay fly) away, (abforpt) in fpeechlefs
     fear!

This place, Thurot, almoft defencelefs found,

And boldly dar'd to tread Hibernian ground:

At Carrickfergus, he a plunder made,

And Belfaft, under contribution laid.

Not till th' Hibernians had their powder fpent,

And from the bafe, their mural hopes had * rent!

                                With

** When thofe who landed from Thurot's fquadron, attack'd Carrickfergus, the few foldiers we had there, with an
                                   heroic

With native zeal! and patriotic glow!

They flung the ramparts * on the charging foe!

Forgetting they expos'd themfelves unarm'd ;

So much the battle had their bofoms warm'd.

So rufh'd unarm'd, the Spartan † from the bath,

Seiz'd on his fpear, and full of martial wrath,

He plung'd amidft the thickeft ranks of foes ;

Who thought fome God had dealt deftructive blows!

They ftood amaz'd†! or join'd the tim'rous rout ;

Whilft he fpread death, and terrors round about!

heroic zeal, and in a moft brave manner, difputed almoft every
inch of ground ; and with a bloody toil, made them dearly buy
their victory! for when all their ammunition was fpent, they
flung the ftones off the ramparts on the advancing enemies!
and held them in play for fome time, as if they had forgotten
the rapid execution of powder and ball ; and that whilft they
demolifh'd the battlements, they left themfelves more expos'd to
the enemy's fhot!

†† This was a Spartan warrior ; who one day happen'd to
be bathing, in a city befieg'd ; when the enemy rufhing fud-
denly and furioufly on, had like to have enter'd triumphantly :
and on hearing the alarm of war, and that the city was like to
be carried by a general affault, he leapt from the bath, laid
hold of his fpear, and plung'd among the charging enemy ; and
dealt his vengeance amongft the thickeft ranks! who feeing him
take fuch deathful ftrides! naked, and unarm'd! inclos'd by a
brazen, iron, and fteely war! fuperftitioufly thought fome deity
had affum'd a human fhape, to fling deftruction thro' their cohorts! and turn the fway of battle! they ftood transfix'd, with
a religious awe! fell unrefifting, beneath his oft tranfpiercing
fpear! or join'd the general rout, as he ftrode to different parts
of the field, and chang'd the fcene of action!

As

As ſtood at gaze, the halting * half ſcar'd Gauls!

Midſt daſhing ſhow'rs, of Carrickfergus walls!

From engines, mortars, ſlings, nor cannon flung!

But from Hibernian nerves, for warlike action ſtrung!

Thus in a thick deſcending ſtony ſhow'r!

They fought 'gainſt numbers, and ſuperior pow'r!

The charging ſhocks, themſelves, like ramparts bore!

Till they cou'd rend the ſtubborn walls no more!

Then like the troops at Cas †; they ſullen frown'd!

And flung their uſeleſs muſkets to the ground!

Not till like them, they'd well the fight ſuſtain'd!

And from the victors, almoſt vict'ry gain'd!

* When the French found themſelves ſo reſolutely oppos'd, by our handful of men at Carrickfergus, after all their ammunition was ſpent: they halted in a ſort of a half ſcar'd gaze, as if in ſuſpence, whether they ſhou'd advance, ſtand the charge, of thoſe few brave men, or make a ſhameful retreat: and doubtleſs, one or two rounds more f Hibernian rhetorick, wou'd have rais'd the pannic to ſuch a height, as to have confirm'd them in an inſtant reſolve, and have made them retire in confuſion!

† It is well known, how fiercely and reſolutely our troops at Cas fought; being about fifteen hundred on ſhore, againſt eleven battalions; (and they on friendly ground:) and likewiſe, with what reluctance they ſubmitted to an overpowering enemy, when all their ammunition was expended.

The

The news no fooner reach'd our half ftarv'd foes,

Our freeborn troops, and brave militia rofe,

Than like a herd of deers, with timid mind,

And hungry wolves, in clofe purfuit behind;

From Ireland's fhorcs, they fled in hafte away,

Quick reimbark'd, and weigh'd, and put to fea!

And thought (o'erjoy'd!) to make their native⎤

    fhore;

With conqueft flufh'd, and fed with Englifh ftore!

But Thurot firft muft fall, and hundreds more!

So once, Amalekites, weak Ziklag fpoil'd;

But David's breaft with manly ardour boil'd!

He chac'd, and fought, and kill'd, retook the prey!

Their triumph damp'd, in death, and cold difmay!

Now Clements, Logie, Elliott, brave, bore down,

To meet Thurot, with formidable frown!

With wonted rage, like England's naval Sons,

They fought, huzza'd, and ply'd Britannia's guns!

                                   Stern

Stern Æolus*, began the rough attack!

And flung (untrimm'd) their bloated fails aback.

Onward he came, in a moft direful form!

And roar'd tremendous! in a fulph'rous ftorm!

Thro' ev'ry fhip, a pannic fright prevails:

The tacks grew ufelefs, as the flutt'ring fails.

In Brilliant † trim, war's mighty gooddefs ‡ frown'd!

She roar'd in flame! and death was in the found!

Elliott, and Clements, and Logie, grew warm;

And near Thurot, they roll'd the loud alarm!

(Thurot, whom (tho' a foe,) we fcarcely blame,

Who bears a gen'rous, manlike warrior's name!)

To clofer fight, they eagerly advance,

Rive the French fhips, and check the pride of France!

The fight grew hot, thick flew the Englifh balls;

And death flew fore and aft, among the Gauls:

The brave, the rafh Thurot, became his prey!

And terror fill'd the French, with dread difmay!

---

* The fhip Æolus, and Æolus is the God of the winds.

† The fhip Brilliant, one of the three which engaged Monfieur Thurot's fquadron.

‡ The fhip Pallas, who with the Æolus and Brilliant, engag'd Thurot's fquadron. Pallas is the Goddefs of war.

As

As twice of late, when Boſcawen, and Hawke, ⎤
Midſt fulminating tars! and clouds of ſulph'rous ⎟
    ſmoke! ⎬
To Conflans, and De Clue, in Britiſh thunder ſpoke! ⎦
Their guns grew mute, they all for quarter call'd,
And down (in fear,) the Gallic enſigns haul'd.
Again they come, and tread our fatal coaſt;
Dejected, maim'd, and all their plunder loſt.

Lewis! be warn'd, and ſend thy men no more,
To tread Hibernia's, or Britannia's ſhore.
Whilſt Hawke, Boſcawen, Holmes, and Saunders
    roam,
Abroad for fame; and Pitt commands at home!
Whilſt England owns ſo many gallant tars!
And brave commanders, for the naval wars!
Whilſt Scotchmen, can their dreaded broad ſwords
    wield!
With Engliſh, and Hibernians, take the field,
Who with their leaders brave, at danger ſmile!
Firm leagu'd, like troops of death, to guard our
    iſle!
                        Whilſt

Whilft Britons ferve great GEORGE, with filial fear,

Who with his Son, and brave old Ligonier,

At Dettingen, like lions, fierce in fight!

Routed main corps, and put gens d'armes to flight!

Whilft King, andP eers, and Council, hand in hand,

Back'd by the body of the nation ftand;

Refolv'd to fave wives, children, lands, and laws!

And Heav'n Propitious, fmiles upon the caufe!

Thy men, as well, may fafely think to tread,

Nightly unarm'd, thro' Africa's dread fhade;

Where lions, tygers, pards, (fierce beafts of prey,)

Roar in the pafs, and dam the dang'rous way,

As e'er expect, in France, to make their boaft,

We victors came, from Britain's dreaded coaft!

As when the riving bolts, are fiercely hurl'd,

By Jupiter, to fcourge the rebel world;

From ftrong Olympus' height, the thunder growls!

And wrapp'd in flame æthereal, onward rolls!

Like eagle mounted Jove, in awful form!

GEORGE, againft Gaul, directs the thund'ring ftorm!

His

His Son, and Grandfons, Bleffings to this land!

Are like the Bolts, uplifted in His Hand!

Eaft, weft, north, fouth, with rapid fpeed He flies,⎤

The Lords and Commons, venerable wife! ⎬

May well be call'd, His eagle's watchful eyes. ⎦

His body, neck, and mighty fweeping tail,

The triple union, Britain's common weal.

To His ftrong pinions, we may well compare,

The Honeft Pitt! and Brave old Ligonier!

The Tars, and Troops, His talons may be call'd,

By whofe ftrong gripe, proud Gallia's fides are
gaul'd!

As with his bill, he feizes tim'rous hares,

Crufhes their bones, and them in pieces tears,

Brave Hawke, and Bofcawen, in pieces break

The Gallic fleets, and may be call'd His beak!

End of B O O K V.

The

The French in Canada, (like a man wash'd from a wreck at sea, and striving to gain the shore:) emerging from the wreck of fifty-nine, as if resolv'd on conquest; and to perform something greatly memorable. Their armament in the spring of sixty, and march towards Quebec; join'd by the savage people in league with them. General Murray, with our other heroic commanders, and troops, rousing to battle. The disposition of our troops, and by whom headed. The closing of the battle. Major Dalling's behaviour. Him and his officers wounded, and his men rushing on without them, driving the enemy, first broken to their main corps, and after to the rear of their army. The French attack on our right. Capt. Ince distinguish'd, with Otway's, and the French twice bravely sustain'd and repuls'd! the left dispossess the enemy from two redoubts. The reserve brought into action. Roufillon's regiment marching up, and penetrating. General Murray's retreat. Due distance kept by the French. The friendly, (daring) action of an Irish serjeant of Bragg's, left wounded on the field of battle, to preserve an English volunteer from being scalp'd by six Indians. He kills three, and the other three flee. A French officer endu'd with humanity; defends him from the other savages; and that they may not kill them as they threaten'd, he sends both into Quebec. The French attack Quebec, but in vain. The gallant defence made by our troops. The arrival of Commodore Swanton, and the Captains, Schomberg, and Dean. Their attack of the French frigates, &c. above the town, and destroying them. The French desert their trenches, and leave ammunition, baggage, field pieces, mortars, tools, &c. &c. &c. A savage nation joins in league with Great Britain.

WAR:

W A R:

B O O K VI.

NOW like a man fatigu'd, and wanting breath,

Wafh'd from a wreck, incircled round
with death :

Who plunging on, amid the furging roar;

Rais'd on a wave, beholds the welcome fhore.

The land he views, with eager longing eyes !

With efforts ftrong, each nerve he nimbly plies ;

More brifkly fwims, as if before untir'd,

In hopes to gain the landing place defir'd :

But foon deprefs'd, beneath a boift'rous wave ;

He flacks, defpairs, and feeks a watry grave !

So Gauls, emerging from the dreadful wreck
Of fifty-nine, advanc'd towards Quebec.
As if forgetting, what they'd lately felt;
The veng'ance, Amherst, Wolfe, and Saunders
    dealt !
Refolved feem'd at first, the war to wage,
As if infpir'd with new heroic rage!
But recollecting Wolfe ! and fifty-nine !
They foon grew cool, and quitted their defign.

The fpring arriv'd ; the gath'ring troops of France
With eager fpeed, towards Quebec advance.
And to the war, (from wild Canadia's lands;)
They drew the fierce, the favage fcalping bands !
Their near approach, our garrifon alarms !
And Murray, Frafer, Burton, rous'd to arms !
Burton ! whofe zeal burft forth in flaming glow !
Midft piercing cold ! midft chilling froft, and fnow !
Active t' infatuate, and counteract the foe !

The brave Macdonald, march'd the foe t' engage;

Who refcu'd Peyton * from Canadian rage.

With thefe, bold Ince, and Dalling, fally'd forth;

Pleas'd with the war! and full of martial worth!

Scotch, Englifh, Irifh, by thefe heroes led;

Moft bravely fought! and for their country bled!

Frafer the brave! in war's dread fcience fkill'd!

Led Highland troops, and Townfhend's to the
   field.

Lafcelles's, and Kennedy's, with Frafer came; ⎫
                                               ⎪
In queft of death, or elfe of deathlefs fame! ⎬
                                               ⎪
Thefe the left wing compos'd, and gain'd a glo- ⎪
                                               ⎭
   rious name!

The daring Murray, (with a ftern delight,)

His troops furveys, and ruminates the fight!

---

* Capt. Macdonald, (a Scotch gentleman,) at the unfuccefsful landing at Quebec, was the means of faving Mr. Peyton,
(an Irifh gentleman,) from about 30 Indians, marching down
to fcalp him after the battle. See the Britifh Magazine of Jan.
1760, and my fiege of Quebec.

Alert

Alert they ftood, with animating glow!

(Unfhock'd at death! and wont to beat the foe !)

They numbers fcorn'd! and onward march'd elate!

As if they'd outface death! and ravifh mighty fate!

Serenely brave! each foldier feem'd to know

'Tis courage aims, and ftrikes the conq'ring blow!

Quebec's great conq'ror, Murray's bofom fir'd!

And Wolfe tho' dead, each warrior's foul infpir'd!

So from the flaming neft, old poets fing,

Another phœnix, ftretches on the wing.

Now front, to front, they clos'd the battle rag'd!

Where Dalling's corps, confpicuoufly engag'd!

Fiercely the French the Britifh charge fuftain!

Till backward forc'd, (like chaff,) they fpread the

    plain.

Onward the foldiers rufh, unaw'd by fear,

And leave their wounded * leaders in the rear!

* Here Major Dalling, and feveral of his officers were wounded ; but his men rufh'd on without 'em, and drove the enemy,
they firft attack'd to the main corps, and afterwards to the rear.
For a full account of this, and the whole battle, vide General
Murray's letter to Mr. Secretary Pitt, in the Extraordinary
Gazette, which contains a perfect account of the whole action,
according to the following lines.

                                Chace

Chace as they flee! advance as they retire!
Oppose the French main corps, and take the gen'ral
	fire!
Again they rally, charge, again retreat
Back to the rear, and own the rout compleat!

Now on our right, their main corps made attack,
Attempted twice, and twice, were driven back!
The great foul'd Murray, deigns this truth to own!
There Otway's fought, brave Ince diftinguifh'd
	fhone!
Amherft's, Americans, were there difpos'd;
With Anftruther's, and Webb's; thefe the right
	wing compos'd;
Stood firm as fate, (unfhock'd,) when twice the
	battle clos'd!

Mean while, the left, with emulating glow,
From two redoubts, they difpoffefs'd the foe.

K 4   Indians,

Indians, Canadians, Regulars repel!

Victorious chac'd! or vanquifh'd, bravely fell!

The * center, and referves, their ftation chang'd;

Advanc'd and wheel'd, in diff'rent order rang'd.

Our little army, none inactive knew;

Each felt the fhock, as warm the battle grew!

Ten thoufand French, by favages fuftain'd,

Three thoufand Britons charg'd, and long the fight

    maintain'd!

Thus like two fcales, with equipond'rous weight,

Both parties toil'd, to fix the doubtful fight.

The Englifh troops, (to battle much inur'd,)

The oft repeated charges firm endur'd:

With minds refolv'd, call'd all their ardour forth;

And made the Frenchmen feel their warlike worth!

The wounded dropp'd, another ftraight appear'd,

Sent leaden fate, or elfe a broad fword rear'd!

* N. B. About this time, the third battalion of Royal Americans, from the referve, and Kennedy's from the center, were
brought up to the action. Vide Gen. Murray's letter, and account of the battle.

Now

Now Rouffillon's * march'd up to frefh attack,

Pierc'd like a wedge, and bore the Britons back.

As growling lions, on Arabia's plain,

Hunters, and dogs, in flow retreat fuftain;

So Murray and his troops, by might born down,

March flowly off, and fierce defiance frown!

As flow the French advanc'd, (as if in fear,)

Due diftance kept, nor dar'd to charge the rear:

Dear bought experience, made their forces feel,

Th' effect of bay'net fight, and Highland fteel!

To where a Briton, and Hibernian lay,

Six fcalping plund'rers, thither bent their way.

Th' Hibernian † rous'd, the favages drew near,

To feize, and fcalp, an Englifh volunteer.

* A French regiment of Rouffillon, which penetrated.

† This was an Irifhman, a ferjeant of Bragg's, who had received a fhot in the breaft, and cou'd not retreat with the reft; who fell'd two of the Indians at one blow, with his halbert; and with a fecond blow kill'd a third; as fix of them were about to fcalp an Englifh volunteer, which lay near him, with a dangerous wound in his leg; and on three being kill'd, the other three fled. This is by letters from America in the news.

Like

Like gallant Peyton *, in the barb'rous ftrife,

To fave his friend's, brave Ochterlony's life ;

His weapon launch'd, transfix'd two Indians thro'! ⎫

Like Jove's own bolt, afkance, the halbert flew! ⎬

The fecond blow, another favage flew! ⎭

Tho' thrice his number, ftill unwounded ftood,

The fanguin'd halbert, chill'd their vital blood !

They cow'r'd beneath the blow, (with abject fear!)

As † Turnus, when Æneas launch'd his fpear !

To flight, (like genuine cowards, quick they yield,)

And leave th' Hibernian conq'ror on the field !

Perchance there ftood, within th' Hibernian's call,

A gen'rous great foul'd foe ! a humane Gaul !

Who with his corps, (quite void of hoftile wrath;)

Travers'd the field of carnage, blood, and death.

---

* The intrepid behaviour of Capt. Ochterlony, and Lieut. Peyton, is mention'd in the unfuccefsful landing at Quebec. The whole ftory may be read at large in the Britifh Magazine of Jan. 1760, and in my fiege of Quebec.
† In the Æneid, 'tis faid, Turnus cow'r'd in fear, when Æneas launch'd his fpear at him, in combat, before the walls of Laurentum in Italy.

To

To him he * call'd; and begg'd he'd fave their lives,

From favage rage, and Indian fcalping knives !

In anxious fort, to him, his arms he rear'd,

Who turn'd, and faw, and touch'd with mercy heard!

As Sol's bright blaze, difpels the fhades of night,

He frown'd, forbid, turn'd human brutes to flight.

Bleft with a foul, compaffionate and mild !

He fmooth'd his brow, and full of pity fmil'd !

To make the act compleat, he ftopp'd not here,

But order'd dreffing, and a decent care.

And then, to make the favage threat'ning vain,·

(Who vow'd revenge for fcalping kinfmen flain,

From chofen Gauls, (the favages to check,)

Murray receiv'd them fafely at Quebec.

* After the ferjeant had lain three of the Indians dead, and the other three fled; he call'd to a French officer which ftood near him, with many of his men, and begged he would be fo good as to protect them from being barbaroufly murdered in cool blood by thefe barbarians. (For there were feveral parties ftill fcouting round the field, ftripping the dead, and murder-ing, mangling, and fcalping the wounded, according to their ufual cuftom.) The officer very generoufly protected them, and ordered them to a place of fafety ; and to preferve them from being butcher'd by the favages in the French army, (who with the greateft indignation and cruel wrath, vow'd revenge for their brothers ;) he next day fent them under a proper guard into Quebec. A noble inftance of French politenefs ! and ho-ftile generofity !

Had

Had Richlieu been like him, politely brave !

Orphans at Zell, had fcap'd a flaming grave !

Mean while, our troops, back to the fort retir'd ;

'Gainft which the foe, (with hard earn'd conqueft

 fir'd,

Indians, Canadians, and the well train'd Gauls,) ⎫

With vain attempt, ply'd ufelefs bombs, and balls ; ⎪

Murray commanded there ! and Britons mann'd ⎬

 the walls ! ⎭

Englifh, and French, engag'd with mutual hate ;

And guns, and mortars, belch'd alternate fate :

With hardy troops, Quebec was amply ftor'd :

And on the ramparts, fix fcore cannon roar'd !

All ftand the teft, like links, in one great chain,

Ward off the threaten'd fate, and well the fiege

 fuftain !

Now Swanton, Schomberg, Dean, approach'd the

 walls ;

Brought Murray joy ! but terrors to the Gauls !

         Ready

Ready for war, with wonted naval glow,

And great vivacity, they fought the foe.

With Englifh fpeed, above the town they glide ;

Their fouls anticipate the rapid tide !

And fafcination flies from each portending fide!

When Britain's flag beyond the walls appear'd,

With pannic ftruck, the daftard Frenchmen fear'd,

Like wax their hearts became, or melting fnow,

And fhipwreck chofe, rather than fight the foe.

Brave Swanton, Schomberg, Dean, each active

    tar,

Roll'd on aftern, in gloomy thund'ring war !

In piftol fhot, next board and board, they came ;

And hurl'd Great Britain's fierce deftructive flame!

A quadrate ruin, 'gainft the Gauls confpires ;

Rocks, water, tars, and black fulphureous fire !

Eager for fight, to grapple with the foe !

Refolv'd to ftrike, a home, deciding blow ;

The galiant Dean, abforpt in warlike flame !

To fhipwreck fteer'd, and gain'd a lafting fame.

As if the French, were acted by one foul,

Or fympathetic fate had rul'd the whole ;

The troops on fhore, (o'erwhelm'd with mighty

    dread,)

In filent terror, from their trenches fled !

Precipitate, retrod their former path ;

At Jacques, fhelter'd from the Britifh wrath !

Field pieces, mortars, powder, fhells, and fhot ;

Provifion, baggage, tools, were all forgot !

Murray with unexpected joy, furvey'd

The camp, with Gallic wealth profufely fpread !

And heaps, on heaps, (tenfold,) his former lofs

    repaid * !

---

* When firft General Murray march'd out with his troops, to meet and oppofe the French, marching towards Quebec ; in his retreat he left feveral field pieces behind. But now he found in the enemy's abandon'd camp, fo many field, or battering pieces, fo much baggage, provifion, ammunition, &c. of every fort, as wou'd make almoft a tenfold retribution.

    Such

Such was their fpeed! fuch their internal fear!

That Murray cou'd not overtake the rear!

A favage nation, (to our rage expos'd,)

In friendly league, with conq'ring Britain clos'd *.

* Whoever reads the extra Gazette, which contains the letter from General Murray, (governor of Quebec,) to Mr. Secretary Pitt, concerning the French fiege of Quebec and raifing
the fiege; with the battle between his and their troops; will I
believe, on the perufal find, that the encomiums which General Murray was generoufly pleafed to give, to the brave and indefatigable Mr. Burton, Frafer, Dalling, Ince, and Macdonald;
and to the bold and active Commodore Swanton, and the Captains, Schomberg and Dean, and to all the troops and tars in
general: I fay I believe they will find what he there fays, to
agree with what I have faid in my poem of the fame. And
that the difpofition for the battle, was as I have faid, under the
fame leaders, whom he exprefsly fays headed the different corps,
or battalions, (if I may fo call them;) for the regiments were
greatly thinn'd. And they will find in his letter, that fuch
events happen'd, fuch attacks, and fuch repulfes, and every
other incident, as I have mention'd; except that of the Irifh
ferjeant of Bragg's, and the Englifh volunteer, left wounded on
the field of battle; which was in the news, and faid to be by
letters from America.

BRITANNIA's CALL

TO HER

Brave TROOPS and hardy TARS.

I.

BRITANNIA's fons, Hibernia's youth,
    And Scotia's hardy, martial race!
    Rife! fight! defend the caufe of truth!
    And wipe from me all foul difgrace!
With ardent eyes,
      Britannia cries,
  United rife!
And Frenchmen to deftruction chace!

II.

See, from the coaft of threat'ning France,
  With mifchief fraught, and ill defigns,
Her gath'ring troops prepare t' advance,
  And threat with battle my confines!

                   Infulting

Infulting foes,..

Refolv'd oppofe,

Deal mortal blows !

See, fee, aloft, my ftandard fhines.

III.

My freeborn fons, (with native rage,)

Arife, and hear your mother's call ;

Invading foes, prepare t' engage :

Defend me now, or elfe I fall :

Your all's at ftake,

To arms betake,

Strong efforts make,

And fweep to death, the troops of Gaul !

IV.

Rouze ! rouze ! refulgent, fhine in arms !

Hark ! cannons roar, drums, trumpets, found!

Rufh on, all clad, in war's alarms !

And dauntlefs, tread, on Gallic ground !

Againft the Gauls,

And their ftrong walls,

Ply bombs and balls,

Fling veng'ance, flame, and ruin round!

Bri-

V.

Britannia thus, befpoke her fons,

  With ardour, ev'ry bofom boil'd,

They lin'd her fhores, with troops, and guns,

  And France, affrighted, back recoil'd:

    With ftern delight,

        They all unite,

    And wifh the fight ;

But Ferdinand had Lewis foil'd !

VI.

A grand exulting joy appear'd,

  With martial fmiles, on England's fhore,

To fee Great Britain's ftandard rear'd,

  And hear her naval lions roar;

    Her fleets France found,

        Were gath'ring round,

    A dreadful bound !

Britannia, heard her threats no more.

VII.

Brunſwick with mighty joy ſurvey'd,

   Domeſtick troops begird his throne ;

Safety her golden wings diſplay'd.

   And all our former fears were flown :

      Our forces good,

         Reſolved ſtood,

      To ſpill their blood,

Sooner than Frenchmen conq'rors own.

Britain's Arms victorious ; or, France humbled.

I.

TO inſults long, from France inur'd,

   Britannia rouz'd, and dreadful frown'd!

Her navy mann'd, her coaſts ſecur'd,

   And fear did ev'ry foe confound !

      Great Heav'n thought fit,

         The patriot Pitt,

      At helm ſhou'd ſit,

And point her flaming veng'ance round.

Her

II.

Her daring troops, Britannia ſcann'd,
    Which faithful ſtood, to guard her ſhore;
Well pleas'd, ſhe ſaw her navy mann'd;
    And heard 'em loud defiance roar:
            Aloud ſhe cries,
                    France ſtill defies,
            Riſe warriors, riſe!
    And drown all Gaul in Gallic gore!

III.

My naval ſons, againſt the Gauls,
    Launch forth, and with a ſtern diſdain,
Tranſport my thunders, to their walls,
    And roll my terrors o'er the main;
            Great George defend,
                    Fiercely contend,
            Make Gallia bend,
    Reſtrain the frog, and check proud Spain.

No

IV.

No longer let proud Gallia boaft,
  But now equipt, and rous'd to arms,
Return the war along their coaft,
Whilft ardour ev'ry bofom warms!
    Their hearts all fail,
        Cold fears prevail,
    Now, now, fet fail!
And fill all France with dread alarms!

V.

Tho' Lewis threats with naval force;
  To view difplays his warlike ftores!
Tho' gath'ring troops, of foot, and horfe,
  Range dreadful, on the hoftile fhores!
    They ardour lack!
        Their threats fling back!
    Their coafts attack!
'Tis thus, Britannia you implores!

VI.

To battle quick, her armies rufh'd,
 The terror of her arms difplay,
With conqueft oft, the troops were fiufh'd,
 Her fleets launch'd forth, and fwept the fea!
   They ev'ry where,
     Stern veng'ance bear,
   Spread death, and fear,
And Gallia felt a dread difmay!

VII.

Thus whilft our fleets fweep o'er the main,
 And troops domeftic guard the fhore,
Tho' France unite with haughty Spain,
 And Holland too, we'll fear no more;
   Their pow'rs we'll meet,
     And roughly greet,
  Whilft Britain's fleet,
In flaming death, fhall loudly roar!

On

✕✕✕✕✕✕✕✕✕✕✕✕✕✕✕✕✕✕✕✕✕✕✕✕

On Monſieur Thurot's deſcent and defeat.

I.

Y E Britons! attend, you ſhall hear how Thurot,
   (He led, only Frenchmen, intirely forgot,)
Tyger like, for awhile, kill'd, ravag'd, and then,
Victoriouſly thought to have ſlunk to his den!

      Derry down, down, down derry down.

II.

With three, or four ſhips, Monſieur Thurot made
      boaſt,
He'd make a deſcent on Hibernia's coaſt:
Next thought to retreat, with his men, and his prey,
As well he might 'ſcape from fierce lions away!

      Derry down, down, down derry down.

For

III.

For Æolus*, blew a ſtrong blaſt in his face!

Flung his ſails all aback†, retarded his pace!

With a brilliant‡ air, mix'd with fierce martial rage,

The Goddeſs‖ of war, ſhe bore down to engage!

Derry down, down, down derry down.

IV.

The Frenchmen grew pale, when they ſaw the three

ſail,

Their paſſage obſtruct, as from Ireland they ſteal;

With vocal huzzas, to Belleiſle's volunteers,

They play'd a rough concert of old Engliſh airs!

Derry down, down, down derry down.

V.

Of the ſymphony rude, the Gauls did complain,

And ſwore the whole tune, was a diſſonant ſtrain!

Their loud ſhouts victorious! their triumphs were

drown'd!

By deep noted baſs, of our cannons around!

Derry down, down, down derry down.

* The ſhip Æolus, and Æolus, is God of the winds.
† Aback, is a ſea term.
‡ The ſhip Brilliant.
‖ The ſhip Pallas, Goddeſs of war.

The

VI.

The fport rougher grew! and the Frenchmen grew
    fick!
Death flew fore and aft, as the bullets flew thick!
Their great hero Thurot, fell wounded, and dead!
Soon after they ftruck, in a cold pannic dread!

        Derry down, down, down derry down.

VII.

Monfieurs! take advice, put an end to thefe wars,
You cannot engage with our troops, and brave tars!
Nor dare near the den of the lion to roam!
Brave Hawke fcours the feas! and great Pitt is at
    home!

        Derry down, down, down derry down.

On

On the heroic Taylors, belonging to Elliot's light horfe, who fought fo. bravely in Germany.

I.

WHEN Granby the brave! (a difciple of Mars!)
Rufh'd forth from Great Britain, to Germanic wars!
(To fight the foe rang'd, or to force the ftrong trench,)
And help Ferdinand 'gainft the fwaggering French!
 Derry down, down, down derry down.

II.

The Taylors, regardlefs, of death, wounds, and fcars!
Refolv'd to leave ftitching, and live by the wars!
With a patriot zeal, they deferted their boards!
Beftrode the war horfes, and brandifh'd their fwords!
 Derry down, down, down derry down.

The

III.

The news throughout England, no fooner was
    known,
What great emulation the Taylors had fhown!
But they lifted in fcores, 'gainft Britannia's foes!
And Elliot's light horfe, was the cohort they chofe!
       Derry down, down, down derry down.

IV.

Behold they fet fail, from their own native land,
And meet a good welcome from brave Ferdinand;
Who led 'em ftraightway, where the foe rang'd in
    view,
They kindled with ardour! and refolute grew!
       Derry down, down, down derry down.

V.

They loaded, and prim'd, and ramm'd home their
    balls;
Set fpurs, and full gallop, they drove on the Gauls!

Face

Face to face they difcharg'd, unfheath'd to engage!

And hew'd thro' the French with Achillean * rage!

Derry down, down, down derry down.

VI.

Gallant Erfkine, the bold! he headed this band!

Who follow'd like death! at the warrior's command.

The French turn'd their backs, broke, fcatter'd,
and fled!

The Taylors rufh'd on, over mountains of dead!

Derry down, down, down derry down.

VII.

Poor Lewis, muft furely be in a fad plight!

When his fwaggering heroes, our Taylors can't
fight!

If before them o'erpow'r'd, in pannic they flee!

How dreadful! muft Great Britain's heroes all be!

Derry down, down, down derry down.

* In the battle, after the death of Patroclus, Achilles gave
no quarter; and even deftroy'd the twelve prifoners he took in
fight, as a facrifice to the manes of his dear Patroclus! and
as the Taylors made fuch flaughter, and gave no quarter! they
might be faid to hew thro' the ranks with Achillean rage!

In

VIII.

In a different fenfe, th' old proverb * we'll take;

Nine foldiers of Gaul, fcarce a light horfeman make;

With feminine tremor! the French are all fmitten!

For nine, dare not face a brave ftitch † of Great

Britain!

Derry down, down, down derry down.

* The proverb is, nine Taylors make a man, by way of flur on them; but now I have inverted it, and faid, nine Frenchmen dare not fight an Englifh Taylor.

† Stitch is a cant word us'd for a Taylor.

F I N I S.

E R R A T A.

Page 14, 2d line, read unparalel'd.

Page 43, 3d line, read Prudent, in Britifh flame moft fiercely flow'd. Since I wrote the poem, I am inform'd it was the .... that burnt that night, and not Entreprenant.

In the reference of page 46, concerning Neftor's advice, read .... on the deed.